PERIL OFF PADRE

Peril Off Padre

Carolyn Hart

ISBN: 979-8-3372-0448-2

This edition published in 2026 by Open Road Integrated Media, Inc.
180 Maiden Lane
New York, NY 10038
www.openroadmedia.com

PERIL OFF PADRE

PROLOGUE

SATURDAY, JUNE 30, 1520

Alonzo lost count of the battles. His body pulsed with pain at every step. His left arm hung crooked and useless. A wound throbbed along his right rib cage. As he hobbled from a lance wound in his right calf, he felt hollow and weak from lack of food. But the pall of misery receded as his right hand reached for gold. No matter the fiery pain as he scrambled for treasure. The Captain General had given the word to move out within the hour. At midnight the Spanish soldiers would battle for survival. The glimmering white city of the lake, which had seemed so magic a world when first glimpsed, was now a watery prison. Outnumbered, surrounded, trapped on the island, they must fight for each inch gained across the causeway. Hordes of Aztec warriors lined the streets and waited in boats along the canals, lances ready. Many Spaniards would die tonight as they fought to cross the causeway, but all would die if they stayed.

When Cortes announced the withdrawal, he threw open the great hall where Montezuma's treasure was stored. Much of the Emperor's gold had been melted down and made into ingots, but the finest of the golden ornaments had been placed in leather chests for shipment to King Charles. Castilian soldiers packed the King's Fifth on stalwart horses.

Alonzo reached for a bar of gold from a stack near the entrance, but those behind him pushed and shoved and swore in thin, strained voices as they struggled to get into the hall.

Alonzo fell forward. A sideways lunge saved him from being trampled. He lost his place and the jostling mass of soldiers grabbed up the ingots and loose pieces of jade. Alonzo had nothing but a bruised hand stamped by a boot. More soldiers pressed forward. Alonzo pulled himself out of the path of more trampling boots. He sought safety in a corner where light from flickering torches didn't reach. As he crawled into the shadows, his hand touched leather. He stiffened. Like a blind man, he traced with his fingers the shape of a sturdy rectangular leather case. The finest pieces were packed in leather cases to ship to the king.

Alonzo's arm closed around the case. His heart thudded so hard he feared the stewards would hear despite the hoarse cries of the soldiers.

Cortes had thrown open the hall, but only after the King's share had been packed and loaded. If Alonzo were caught with a leather case, he would be killed. He crouched on the stone floor and looked wildly about, but no one saw him in the dark corner. No one had eyes for anything other than shining heaps of gold.

Alonzo thrust the case beneath his cloak. He struggled awkwardly to his feet and pushed his way out of the hall.

Rich, rich, rich. He would be rich, rich, rich.

The men, many clutching gold bars, assembled. At midnight, two hundred Spanish feet led the way. The Aztecs had destroyed the bridges across the canals. The soldiers pushed and shoved into place the wooden bridge Cortes had ordered built. As they began to cross, warriors attacked.

Thick clouds obscured the moon. Rain glazed the wooden bridge. Men and horses slipped and fell. Canoes sped across the dark water, warriors hurling spears. If one warrior fell, ten more took his place.

Dead horses and men tumbled into the cold water of the lake. Warriors shouted and whistled and struck. The Spaniards and their allies thrust and parried and struggled forward.

Alonzo fought with the swordsmen in the unit directly behind Cortes. He made it across the temporary bridge over the first canal. Leaning forward, he stumped ahead as quickly as he could on his lamed leg, swinging and jabbing his sword. Sweat ran in rivulets down his face, mingling oddly with cold needles of rain. Beneath his cloak, he clamped his left arm hard against his side, holding the rectangular leather case tight to his body.

The struggle never stopped all the long way westward across the causeway. Alonzo lost track of his friends, Rafael and Tomas. They had fought together under Cortes from Veracruz to the white city of the lake, but now Alonzo was alone in the night. Ahead the *clip-clop* of horses' hooves sounded behind the ragged thump of running feet. Someone cried out, "The shore!"

Alonzo strained his aching chest and drove his leaden legs. The shore. If only he could reach the shore. Suddenly another boat filled with screaming warriors splashed alongside him. He broke into a desperate, ungainly run.

The spear penetrated his back just below the left shoulder blade. His momentum, his desperate will to live, carried him forward. He was almost to the end of the causeway when he toppled into the cold water. His cloak snagged in the roots of a cypress tree and his dead hands locked in final stricture on the leather case.

* * *

SUNDAY, MARCH 26, 1553

Fog swirled over the causeway. Fray Eduardo could see only a few feet ahead, but he clicked his heels against the donkey's side. *"Pronto, pronto, Marguerita. Seramos tarde."*

Marguerita flicked her ears. Impatiently, the priest whacked her in the ribs again. The mule stopped short, her front legs rigid, and he hurtled over her head. As the plump, cassocked priest cannoned through the air, he instinctively began a prayer, "Mary, Mother of God . . ." remembering all the while the soldiers' taunts that his stupid mount would be the end of him and feeling an empty shrinking inside because he didn't know how to swim.

Icy water closed over his head. His arms flailed wildly, propelling him forward into the exposed roots of a cypress tree clinging to the shoreline. A firm grip on the roots eased Fray Eduardo's panic enough for him to blink and look around.

Fog still hung low and thick, glistening in the branches of the cypress tree, but land was there and he was saved. *Grácias a Jesus*, he murmured.

The icy lake water was numbing his body and making his rough woven cassock heavy as armor, so he tightened his grip and tried to pull himself up. His foot was stuck. He wiggled and yanked and jerked but it wouldn't come free. Finally there was nothing for it but to bend over into the water and use his hand to free his sandal from the entangling roots.

He pulled and tugged and then, as his sandal was coming loose, he felt a shifting near his leg and something square pressed against him. He scrambled backwards but something heavy followed. He kicked; the blackish mass came up through the water, and he saw it for what it was—a sodden rectangular box of leather. He forgot his fear, took a firm grip on his discovery, and made his way to shore.

On the bank, he huddled in his thick, wet cassock and tried to unbuckle the leather case. He tugged and pushed, but the clasps wouldn't move. He poked and prodded the case and finally found a deep scratch on the side, as if it had been scored by a sharp blade. The cut hadn't sliced through the leather but his pulls and pokes split the weakened case. What he saw caused him to look quickly about, but no one was near to see.

When he re-mounted Marguerita, his mind was so absorbed that he didn't even think to beat her. He felt the cold weight of the leather case against his chest as the donkey trotted off the causeway and toward the village church where he was expected. The soldiers and Indians who awaited him laid his abstraction during the service to his dunking.

Fray Eduardo thought about his find all that day and the next and the next. He was, at heart, a simple man, eager to do his duty, slow to take offense, quick to kindliness. His superiors never found fault with his devotion and would have said that Fray Eduardo could always be depended upon to do exactly as he ought.

But Fray Eduardo, for all that he was an unworldly missionary priest, felt in his heart that it was wrong to destroy the fabric of Indian life. He shared his superiors' certainty that it was their duty to teach them about Christ, but he did not believe, as so many others in the Church, that it was just as important to uproot and throw away every last vestige of their culture.

If he gave the treasure to his superiors, they would more than likely melt it down into ingots because the delicate and lovely golden pieces were revered religious objects from an Aztec temple.

He knew many of the Aztec gods were evil, with their

unceasing demand for blood and sacrifice, but the pendants and disks and temple utensils had a glory and a beauty his soul ached to protect.

So he made his decision. The Plata Flota, twenty great ships, would leave Veracruz early next month for Spain. He would travel home on the flagship—and the treasure of the Aztecs would go with him.

It was a grave decision. He knew the fate of those who smuggled gold into Spain without the King receiving his fifth. It wouldn't matter that profit was not his motive. Moreover, he had never before deceived his Church.

Fray Eduardo did not rest easy in his decision. He prayed many times, seeking the guidance of his Lord. Later, some who remembered his grave face and long prayers said that he must have had a presentiment.

The fleet sailed on schedule, laden with gold and emeralds, silver and pearls, and even greater treasure than the stewards knew.

Fray Eduardo said mass every morning and the daily offices and the great ships plowed their way to Havana. Three ships went on as advance scouts and then the seventeen set sail for the Florida Straits. They were not far short of the straits when long, steady swells began to sweep broadside to the big ships. The bright blue sky paled and the sun was indistinct behind a gauzy haze.

The long swells grew steeper. The ungainly ships began to roll and flounder in deep troughs. Older seamen grew quiet and stopped complaining about the thick, heavy heat that plastered the clothes to their bodies.

The wind changed direction toward evening, veering from east to north. Then the wind stopped. Swells deepened. The men were very quiet.

When the wind began to pick up, gusts came from the

north-northwest. Clouds mushroomed from scraps of gray mist and soon, black and thick, they hid the setting sun. The rain struck explosively, splatting down so hard and fast a man could see no more than a hand before his face. Waves towered high and higher. Ships rolled heavily. Some were swamped.

Desperate captains turned their vulnerable lumbering ships northwestward and the winds began to speed them toward their fate.

That squall passed as darkness fell but Fray Eduardo was puzzled when the sailors moved about their repairs grimfaced and joyless. The swells did not lesson.

Three more squalls, swift and vicious, battered the disorderly fleet that night, hurling the ships ever nearer the low-lying shallow coast. The hurricane struck just before dawn in a black and awesome world. Wind shrieked around the now widely separated ships. Aboard the flagship, the storm struck savagely, the wind shrilling in a mind-flattening cacophony. The mast splintered. As it split and fell, the sound of destruction could not be heard above the wind. Gigantic waves drove the wounded hulk into the shallow, sandy bottom. The ship ripped and twisted apart as if it had no more substance than a canoe.

Seventeen ships sailed from Havana. Three grievously damaged galleons reached safety. Fourteen perished. Of these, at least three were dashed to pieces against a long narrow island curving off the coast.

SATURDAY, MAY 5, 1979

The day began gloriously. A perfect day. Keith's scuba gear was piled by the apartment door when the phone rang. He picked up the receiver and frowned as he listened. "You're not coming?"

The voice on the other end was a little defensive, but not overly. "I said I'd come if I could, but I can't make it. I've got two papers due before finals."

Keith looked at the scuba gear waiting by the door. He tried again. "I've already got beer in the cooler. I can pick you up in ten minutes."

Jack interrupted. "Two papers, man. Maybe next weekend."

Keith hung up. He couldn't scuba dive alone. He turned and stared out the window at the beautiful clear sky and knew the Gulf would be perfect for diving on such a day.

Diving alone was dangerous. Foolhardy. He'd never dived alone. But he had waited so long for a day such as this, a perfect day to dive. Maybe today would be his lucky day. Ever since he found that gold coin, he'd gone back to that particular stretch of coast. Last September he'd strolled on a deserted beach on Padre Island and found the shiny coin with the face of Charles V. He had stood on the hard-packed sand and gazed at surging water. The coin meant that not far out lay the remains of one of the ships of the fabulous Plata Flota of 1553.

He'd scarcely managed to breathe as he stared at foam-flecked, murky water still yielding debris from the hurricane that had careened across the Gulf the month before.

What a triumph it would be to discover another of the galleons. Some wrecks had been found and pillaged. Even now Texas authorities were still wrangling with a treasure hunting group over ownership of three hundred pounds of artifacts salvaged in 1967.

If he found a wreck, he would apply for permission for his university to excavate. The department would conduct a text-book excavation, everything done right, properly gridded sections, photographs, sketches, recovery of visible artifacts, and painstaking removal of sand with an air hose.

The perfect excavation and he would be one of the youngest archeologists ever to help lead such a project.

All winter long, whenever he could manage a free day, he came to the lonely stretch of beach. His friend Jack, an unworldly philosophy major, had been delighted to help him search. But the Gulf doesn't run to clear waters in the fall and winter and there had never been a day with visibility of more than ten or twelve feet.

Keith looked out his window at the beautiful day, then grabbed up his scuba gear. He still hadn't decided whether he'd dive alone even when as the rented motorboat chugged through Corpus Christi Pass. He took his time lining up his landmarks until he was offshore from the area where he'd found the coin. As he let out the anchor, he looked down into the water and for an instant thought his mind was playing tricks. He leaned closer to the water and saw the long, straight, unmistakable line of a shell-encrusted cannon.

He had found the wreck. It was below him, waiting.

Dangerous to dive alone . . . He was a trained diver, a field archeologist. He was careful. He adjusted his tanks. He checked his face mask, then raised the diver's flag. Even so, as he slipped down into the soft warm water, he felt the uneasiness bred by guilt. He knew he was taking a chance to dive alone.

But this was one dive he had to make.

His uneasiness was swept away in the excitement as he slowly swam over the site. The debris from the galleon must have been thickly covered by sand soon after the wreckage was strewn across the sandy bottom. Noting else could account for the magnificent condition of the coin he had found in September. Now the remains of the wreckage had been newly uncovered by last summer's hurricane.

He swam above great dark lumps that might be fused silver

coins and a mound of rounded balls that had to be ballast. He swam back and forth until he had a clear picture of the entire area. The expedition would, of course, draw and photograph it in every detail, but for now he had a good grasp of the extent of the site

He heard the muffled thrumming of a motorboat passing overhead and thought nothing of it. After all, the diver's flag was out, warning that he was below. A sense of movement from above caused him to lift his head. Another diver was descending. He felt a surge of relief that it wasn't a shark.

The swimmer glided toward him. The diver was a fellow of about his own age with a thick neck and heavy shoulders. A strong muscular swimmer.

The intruder, for that was how Keith saw him, was swimming closer and closer. There was something purposeful, even inimical, in that steady approach.

He reached Keith, stopping an arm's length away. Then, his meaning clear, he jabbed his finger sharply at Keith, half-turned to spread his hand in an arc indicating the wreckage, then pointed at himself. He could not have made himself better understood with a thousand words. It was surprising, too, how much violence of emotion the pantomime expressed.

If Keith had not been so excited, so exhilarated by his discovery, so possessive of it, he might not have responded so strongly. As the intruder claimed ownership, Keith violently shook his head.

The intruder stared at Keith for a long moment, then he moved. He pulled free a knife sheathed to his leg. With one upward stroke, he sliced an arc through the water and through Keith's air hose.

Keith stared in stupid fascination at the bubbles spewing upward, thousands of air bubbles. Then his air was gone. The only air he had was what was in his lungs. For a tiny instant, panic touched him, then he regained his nerve and began to stroke upward, knowing that he had plenty of time to reach the surface. All he had to do was rise slowly and gradually exhale.

At first, the grip on his ankles was just another impediment to overcome. He looked down. The stocky young man was holding his ankles. Suddenly, violently, Keith was angry. Damn the man. First he'd cut his hose and now he'd grabbed his ankles. Keith struggled, tried to kick. The grip tightened.

He struggled, air gone, pulling suffocating salt water into his lungs. Soon after, his body sank onto the ocean floor to rest over the shell-encrusted cannon.

CHAPTER 1

Judy Martin had lived twenty miles from the Gulf her entire life, but she had never been on a boat until Harry asked her. The past few weeks had been the most wonderful she had ever known. She hugged to herself the secret of her Wednesday afternoons. She didn't care that Harry paid little attention to her on the boat because the secret hours expanded her world. She loved every minute she spent out on the bright water.

She was a little frightened of him at first. He was so stocky and bull-like. She had rarely been around men and never anyone like Harry. She remembered the whispers of the girls huddled behind the honeysuckle shrubs at the church camp, and she remembered the boy Willie who asked her to sneak out of her tent late one night and meet him down at the baseball diamond and his hot hesitant hands and how she had run back up the twisting path and never looked at him again.

Everything had been an exciting blur since she turned eighteen and left the last foster home. They'd been nice enough, but Mrs. Cooper was always tired and behind. She'd wished Judy well, warned her about men, told her she was a good worker, and to look for a housekeeping job. Judy wanted to see the ocean. She hitched a ride and ended up in Aransas Pass. She was thrilled when she got a job at Nightingale Courts, an old motel which had been remodeled to efficiency apartments. Bailey was the owner and she ran a little café at the front of the Courts. Judy worked at the café and also helped old Mrs. Walker clean the units. She had a little room next to the storeroom and a small salary.

Over time she came to recognize the tenants, who often ate at the Courts café in the evenings. The Misses Talbot both smelled very faintly of violets. The sisters had retired from teaching years ago. Eventually they gave up their old three-story house and moved to the Courts. Judy loved cleaning their unit. She admired their elegant belongings: a gray-and-rose petit point chair their mother had brought to Texas from Ohio, a silver-framed wedding photograph of their parents, a little leather trunk that held their baby shoes, an afghan their grandmother had knitted, and albums filled with old, yellowing photographs of people whose names and faces would evoke recognition from no one but Amy and Louisa Talbot. Next to them was Mr. Schank, who worked at Livermore Drugstore. Mr. Schank always smelled strongly of mints and men's cologne. He sat glassy-eyed in the café at dinner and ate very little. After dinner, he walked to the café front door and out to the sidewalk, planting his feet solidly with each step.

Then came Miss Colby, the librarian. Judy wondered how many books she owned. Books were everywhere—on tables, stacked on the floor, in the closets.

Mrs. Frank, a plump, pleasant-faced widow in her late fifties, used her living room space for a sewing machine and the always-full rack of clothes upon which she worked. Mrs. Bailey said she was the best seamstress in Aransas Pass.

Number Five was rented by Harry Cassell. He was much younger than the other tenants and kept to himself. Some of them visited in the café after dinner. He never spoke to anyone.

Next came Mr. and Mrs. Michaels. She was in poor health.

Diffident Mr. Oliver, a salesman at The Shoe Mart, was in the last unit by the alley.

Eventually faces and names sorted out and she learned who used sugar in their tea and which ones wanted milk for their coffee. She never had any trouble remembering Harry Cassell. Right from the very first evening his strong face was distinct among all those faces. He was overwhelmingly masculine. Amid the pallor of the other tenants, the copper gleam of his suntanned skin was almost shocking. His heavy shoulders and broad hands made everyone else seem frail, insubstantial.

It was only in physical presence that he was remarkable. He never spoke unless directly addressed. He ate quickly whatever special was on the menu. He never really seemed to care what was served.

The first few evenings Judy served him warily, all the while flashing quick little looks at his dusky blond hair, his thick bull neck, his broad, tanned face.

He never noticed her. Or if he did, he didn't see her as a girl but as a waitress with as much interest to him as the chair he sat in or the table at which he ate. She didn't realize how much this disappointed her even while the lack of notice reassured her. But the overwhelming maleness that frightened also attracted her. She began to pour his coffee more slowly and lean a little closer as she did.

Whenever Mrs. Bailey talked about him, Judy listened with especial interest. Every evening, Judy washed dishes in the café's suds-filled sink, swiping the cloth across the plates, plunging it into the glasses. Mrs. Bailey stood, heavyset and sweating, dish towel in hand, and slowly dried, talking all the while. She wondered why Mrs. Frank hadn't eaten her pudding and what had been in the airmail letter she received that morning. She speculated on where the Misses Talbot had gone that afternoon at two. "So unlike them, Judy! I must ask Maisie at Sprague's. Perhaps that's where they went." She shook her head and complained at the way Mr. Schank hadn't eaten a bite of the pork roast! Most of the words, rolling in the rhythmical wash of Mrs. Bailey's high-pitched voice, merged with the shush of the water but if Mrs. Bailey offered this or that comment about Harry Cassell, Judy heard.

". . . lucky to have Mr. Cassell. He has a good, steady job, and of course, he's gone so much and that makes less wear on the apartment. He's a truck driver for Pan-Con lines. Mr. Schank was a bookkeeper with them once but he lost his job. . . ."

Judy's mind would hold to Harry Cassell and his thick swirl of hair instead of the big stack of to the dirty pots and pans. One evening or another, she learned a good deal about Harry Cassell. He had lived at Nightingale Courts for almost five years. He wasn't from Aransas Pass. Mrs. Bailey had frowned when she said it. She didn't know where he was from. He had walked in one summer day and said he'd seen her ad in the paper. She knew where he worked because Pan-Con called him for different runs. He worked odd runs since he was single and available. He certainly, Mrs. Bailey said waspishly, minded his own business! Why, he hardly ever stopped to pass the time of day. But he seemed to be a clean-cut young man. There was an implicit hint that all men must have some vice, and of the danger of being taken in by a pleasant appearance. Mrs. Bailey related in an almost disappointed fashion the intelligence that he didn't smoke or drink and was never seen with girls. There were, of course, all those nights when he was on the road. His apartment was always neat except for those tanks of oxygen or whatever and it was hard to keep the sand swept out, but sand was a small price to pay for such a quiet young man. Of course, she didn't like those stacks of magazines, some with covers a lady shouldn't have to see, but still and all, he always paid his rent on time, fifty dollars every Saturday morning on the dot.

Judy listened as she washed dishes, and on evenings when Harry Cassell was in the café, she flicked quick tentative looks at his ever-deepening tan and the glistening golden mat of hair that furred his arms and the back of his hands.

A week before her world grew to include the sweep of the Gulf, she had stopped across the table from him to pick up Schank's plate and she had dared to look straight at Harry. He suddenly looked at her and something moved deep in his light blue eyes. Her gaze fell away first and her cheeks flushed like the ripening blush on a summer peach. Her hands trembled as she carried his plate to the kitchen.

The next Wednesday morning, she perfunctorily knocked on his apartment door, balancing clean sheets under her left arm and turning the key to his room with her right hand. He was always gone by eight-thirty. She unlocked the door and stepped inside. She was closing the door behind her when she saw him sitting in the corner of the room in an overstuffed easy chair.

One foot stumbled over the other and then she was turning, her right hand grasping for the door knob. "I'm sorry. I thought you'd gone. I mean, you always leave early. I'll come back later."

"That's all right," he said in his soft tenor voice with its thick Texas drawl. "You go right ahead."

She hesitated, then hurried to the bed and began to strip it down. She tucked in the bottom sheet and was spreading the top when he said, "I'm Harry Cassell. What's your name?"

"Judy." She plumped up the pillows then reached for the

spread. “Judy Martin.” She darted a quick look at him, sitting big and solid in the chair, watching her.

She worked in silence, felt her face turning pink, knew he looked. When she finished in the bathroom and stepped out, he stood and walked slowly across the room. “You ever get any time off in the afternoons?”

For an instant she gloried in sheer feminine triumph. She tried to answer carelessly, but the words tumbled out in a breathless eager rush. “I clean the apartments in the morning then help out in the café at eleven. Every afternoon I’m off from one to five. I get Wednesdays off all day since I work on Saturday.”

“Every afternoon.” His voice was as light and slow and easy as the spread of honey.

Her head bobbed up and down and her chest ached from her taut-held breath.

“You ever been fishing?”

Her face crumpled into a puzzled frown. She had been so sure he would ask her out. Why did he want to know if she could fish? She was slowly shaking her head when she realized that maybe he wanted to invite her to go fishing. “I’ve never been fishing, but I’d sure like to go. I know fishing must be great. I know I’d like it.”

“You want to come out fishing with me?” Suddenly, his voice was alive and she knew with a satisfied thrill that her answer really mattered to him. He really wanted her to come.

So she shrugged and let her words wait for an instant until she saw the beginnings of a frown on his face before she said casually, “Why, sure. I guess I’d like to do that.”

The tension eased out of his face. “I’ll pick you up at the corner by the bus station at one o’clock”

“Today?” she asked, surprised.

The frown began to pull at his face again and his voice was almost sharp. "Yeah. I got today off, see. I have to go when I can. I need . . ." He broke off. His face smoothed and when he spoke again, his voice wheedled. "See, it's a good day for fishing. Okay?"

"Why sure, Mr. Cassell."

"Harry."

"Why sure, Harry."

The magic of the ocean bewitched her that very first afternoon. She thrilled to the great reaches of water, the tumble-away sensation of staring down into the green-blue depth and seeing far below the shimmering flash of a fish. She loved the soft, salty air and the gentle trickle of sweat that ran down her face, the glow of the sun in the west and the whippy wind. Most of all she loved the fantastic emptiness of the ocean.

Nothing had been quite as she expected it. He had picked her up near the bus station in a beat-up Ford and that had been her first surprise. Somehow she had imagined that a man who drove one of the big cross-country trucks would have a fine car, but his Plymouth had a crumpled right front fender and salt-rusted sides. Two worn and dirty Army blankets were draped on the front and back seats. The back seat was filled by a couple of big silver-colored tanks and a black face mask and a mound of unfamiliar equipment.

At the marina, he ignored her after he parked the car. He bent to the back seat and wrapped the blanket around the tanks. Then he stepped away from the car empty-handed and looked carefully around.

Puzzled, Judy looked, too. A family loaded a sailboat at the next dock. They worked with a lot of good-natured bantering and joking. They paid no attention to Harry and Judy after a casual hello wave.

Farther away a skinny middle-aged man in khakis sat on the dock, mending a net. His eyes fell away when Harry looked at him. Harry stared for a long moment, but when the man's head stayed bent, Harry looked at her, said almost absent-mindedly, "We're here. Come on. The boat's over there," and he gestured at a slip. Then he reached in the car, grabbed up the bundled blanket, and hurried to the boat. He jumped easily onto the afterdeck then disappeared into the small cabin housing.

Judy waited uncertainly on the dock, trying to gauge the gentle swell that lifted the boat close to the dock then away.

Harry came up the steps and gestured for her to jump, so she did, landing heavily on the deck. "Have a seat," he said, pointing at the canvas chairs at the stern. Each was bolted to the deck and each had a metal socket attached to one side.

Judy moved to one of the chairs and sat down but she half-turned in the seat to watch him. He moved easily even though his stocky body looked awkward and heavy on the boat. She looked down into the cabin area. He was stowing the tanks and the mask in a cabinet, then checking the contents of an ice chest. A moment later he stepped up out of the cockpit, muttered, "Gonna get some ice. Be right back," and jumped up to the wooden dock, then strode off toward a green-painted wooden shack about 40 yards up the shore.

He returned with a 20-pound sack of crushed ice, a six-pack of Cokes, and a bucket filled with long, narrow, silver fish. He plunked the bucket down by her. "Bait." He carried the ice to the chest in the cockpit and dumped it in the container, then poked the bottles of Coke down into the ice.

She watched, admiring his muscular arms and the smooth tightness of the tee-shirt across his back.

He was sliding the lid of the ice chest into place when foot-steps sounded on the dock.

The skinny middle-aged man who had been mending the net drew even with Harry's boat and stopped. He looked at them with bright curious eyes. "I see you got ribbon fish for bait. I guess you don't give up easy."

Harry stood very still. His light blue eyes narrowed. "Give up?" His honey smooth voice rose in a soft question.

"You been leavin' this marina a couple months now and I don't guess I've seen you bring back any fish yet. Course, if you do a lot of divin' you don't have much time to fish."

Harry moved up out of the cockpit. "Man, I always got time to fish," he said genially. "And you got me wrong. I don't spear-fish much at all. I don't even have my tanks along." He moved closer to Judy and reached down to pat her on the shoulder. "I brought me along a good luck charm. Man, I'll bet we bring us home a tarpon this afternoon."

Judy was a little surprised at Harry's sudden warmth, but delighted by it. She smiled at the friendly stranger.

Harry was still talking "Sure sorry you didn't come up and say hello last week. I could've shown you my fish. Man, I always catch fish."

"What you been catchin'?" The man asked and Judy was puzzled at the intentness of his faded blue eyes.

"Got two redfish and a mackerel my last time out." Harry shook his big head. "I hooked the biggest hammerhead I ever seen but he wiggled loose. Man, was he big." He stretched his arms wide. "Maybe I'll find him this time." He clapped Judy on the shoulder again. "Time to head out. Take it easy, mister. Nice talkin' to you," and he turned away.

The man said, "Sure thing," but still he stood on the dock and his intent blue eyes darted all around the boat as if searching for something Then his eyes met Judy's and he smiled. "Good fishin', little lady."

“Thank you,” she called.

The motor roared to life then settled into an even rumble as the boat began to move out into the channel.

Once Judy wondered if she ought to join Harry at the wheel but he didn’t call her and she didn’t want to leave her chair. The boat picked up speed and spanked across the waves. Fine sharp spray glittered in the bright sunshine. She forgot about Harry. She was part of the boat, skimming across the water. When they reached the open Gulf and the swells deepened, she gloried in the surge and flow of the water.

She didn’t know how long they traveled. When the motor stopped, she was sharply disappointed. She could have ridden so forever, but she turned to smile at Harry. The smile slipped away.

He wasn’t looking at her. He stood just out of the cockpit, staring across the water. His head turned slowly, very slowly. His eyes scanned the water all the way around the boat.

Judy, too, stared out around the water. When she had looked, she darted a puzzled glance at Harry. There was nothing anywhere but the sea, the bright hard blue of the sea. No land, no boats, no buoys. Only the heaving, limitless sea, and to the west, a sea gull, its wings wide and still, skimming along an air current.

Harry completed his survey, turned to her. “I’ll show you how to fish.”

He was patient. He took one of the narrow silver-skinned ribbon fish and showed her how to snag it solidly to the two hooks at the end of the line. He showed her how to tilt the rod so that the baited and weighted hook pulled the line down into the water without having to cast. He pushed the lever forward and showed her how to press her finger against the running line so it wouldn’t foul and how to pull the lever back to stop the line.

"If you feel a big hard yank," he explained earnestly, "let your line out gradual-like. Keep your finger on the line so it won't tangle. When the fish eases up, reel him in."

She practiced dutifully several times. When he nodded in approval, she felt very proud.

"Now the last thing, if you get a fish and haul him in, he'll be flipping and flopping. You have to hit him with this." He reached down, unhooked a gaff, and handed it to her.

Judy took the mallet gingerly and placed it on the deck next to her chair.

He turned and hurried away.

Busy with the rod, it took her a moment to realize he wasn't settling into the chair next to hers and there was only one fishing rod out. She looked over her shoulder and saw him coming out of the cabin.

He wore black swim trunks. A silver-colored tank was strapped to his back. A mouthpiece with a hose hooked to the tank dangled from his shoulder. He carried a diving mask in his hand.

He stopped beside her. "Judy, I'd sure appreciate it if you'd give me some help. I want to do some diving." He frowned. "I hunt for things in the water. Old things mostly. Things that don't belong to anybody, but if you find stuff, somebody'll try to take it from you. That's the way it always is. Somebody like me finds something and some guy with money gets a smart lawyer and they'll find a way to take it away from you. Do you know what I mean?"

She nodded because that's the way it was. The rich got richer and the poor got poorer, and they'd gig you if they could. Sure. She understood.

Harry stared out across the water. "Finders, keepers," he said harshly. "I hunted for years and it's mine. Nobody's going to take it away from me." He looked down at her. "You can help me a lot. I don't want anybody ever to know I go diving. See, you and me, we'll go fishing and nosy guys won't watch me so close. We'll just go fishing. That's all anybody'll ever know. You can sit out here where everybody can see you."

She shivered a little at his words as she looked around the empty sea.

He gripped her arm "Oh, they come spying on me, watching me. But you and me, we'll fool them. Each time I come up from a dive, I'll knock on the bottom of the boat. You look around, slow and careful. If you see anybody, a shrimper, a sailboat, a launch, anybody, knock hard three times on the deck. I'll stay down. If nobody's here, knock once."

After he slipped over the side and disappeared into the depths, she felt forlorn. He hadn't asked her to go fishing because he liked her. He wanted a lookout. She gave a little shrug, then swung out the rod and tilted it up. She watched the bait slide down through the water in a swirling, curving plummet until she pushed the lever forward and the line held fast. From that moment on, she didn't care why Harry asked her. She discovered deep sea fishing. She was hooked.

She and Harry nosed out into the moving blue world of the Gulf every Wednesday afternoon for a month. This last week, Harry had taken his vacation. Every afternoon they returned to the same place. After Harry slipped over the side of the *Lucky Lady*, she tipped her rod and watched the line run out. Sometimes she rested back in the chair and held the rod and looked lazily around the horizon. Sometimes she stood and stared down into water, glassy one day, murky another. Always she loved the water. Always the hollow thump from the bottom of the boat was an unwelcome intrusion, but dutifully, she checked the horizon and warned him if need be because she was grateful for the glorious solitary hours when she fished. Sometimes when she signaled that no one was near, Harry hauled aboard a heavily-laden basket. At first she was terrifically curious. She tried to get a glimpse of what it was that mattered so much to him. All she ever saw, until that last day, was ugly, dark clumps, some covered over by hundreds of little shells. She thought to herself it was a lot of fuss about nothing. But she didn't say so. Who cared so long as she got to fish?

It was on Monday the first day of Harry's vacation, that a sleek white charter boat, the *Sue Belle* II, came near in the late afternoon, homeward bound from an early morning charter trip. She looked up as the beautiful boat swept past and saw a darkly handsome boy at the wheel. He saw her at the same instant and lifted his hand to wave. She waved back.

On Tuesday afternoon the *Sue Belle* came near again. Judy was standing, furiously reeling in a blue marlin. She dragged the big fish aboard and was clumsily gaffing it when the *Sue Belle* slowed.

"Good catch," the boy shouted. As he moved past, his friendly smile was puzzled because the pretty girl was apparently all alone.

On Wednesday the *Sue Belle* came that way again. This time the boy was alone in the boat. He slowed and idled the *Sue Belle*'s engine.

"You fish every day?"

"This week," she called back.

"You by yourself?"

Judy looked around uncertainly. Suddenly, it occurred to her that Harry might not like this, he might not like it at all.

She shook her head hard. "No, I'm not."

The boy stared at the cabin housing on the *Lucky Lady*.

Judy knew he could likely see the cabin was empty.

"You got a diver out?" He gestured at the water. "I don't see a flag."

Judy just shook her head.

Abruptly a muffled thump sounded. Judy knew Harry was asking her to check. On the quiet placid day she knew the thump was audible to the boy in the charter boat. She glanced down at the bottom of her boat then across the water at the *Sue Belle.* Abruptly, she leaned down and knocked three times on the deck. She raised her head almost defiantly and called, "Please. You'd better go now."

"Is everything all right?"

"Yes. Please go," She knew without knowing why *Sue Belle* should go.

The boy shrugged and swung the *Sue Belle* away and upped his speed until his wake spread wide and high.

On Thursday the *Sue Belle* approached slowly, easing to a stop about fifty yards off the stern.

Judy saw him, saw his wave. But she didn't give an answering wave. She turned her head away.

He watched for a moment longer then he opened up the throttle and the *Sue Belle* whipped in front of the Lady Luck and the Sue Bell's wash rocked the smaller boat.

Harry, his eyes barely above the surging water, floated in the dark shadow off the port bow. He watched the *Sue Belle* until she was nothing more than a blur on the horizon.

CHAPTER 2

Lee sketched rapidly, trying to capture the self-assured aura of the gleaming boat berthed at the slip almost directly across the road. She held the pencil poised above the half-done drawing, wondering exactly how the motor cruiser achieved its image. It was not the largest craft in view. It was large enough and probably cost a shocking sum, but it wasn't size that made the boat distinctive.

She glanced around the Port Aransas marina. Sport fishing boats, yawls, sloops, and motorboats moved gently up and down in the bright blue water. Most were attractive and well-cared for, but none had quite the air of the *Sue Belle* II. The gleaming white cruiser was as self-confident and poised as a beautiful woman, beautifully gowned.

Lee's hand dropped again to the page. Swiftly the boat took shape on the paper. She was blocking in the wide expanse of windows on the flying bridge when she heard the jaunty toot of a ferry approaching the island. She paused to look across the channel. She had never seen anything quite like the ferries that served Mustang Island. She smiled as she watched the approach. The strange little craft looked absurd, like a square plate with a little house tucked on top of a slender supporting column near the stern. Cars and trucks rode on the plate and the captain stood in the little square house and steered.

She watched until it docked, then turned to look again at the *Sue Belle*. She studied the sketch. Her eye had seen far more and far better than her hand had drawn. Which was, of course, why she taught English (Kipling her specialty) in a modest junior college and was not an artist with portfolio. Or even without, for that matter.

It was still fun to try. It felt good to hold a sturdy thick-leaded pencil and feel its vigorous progress across the grainy manila paper and to see a drawing take shape, the shape she chose.

She stopped for a moment to shade her eyes from the sun and wished she had remembered to bring along her beach hat. But she was almost finished and then she'd drive back to the cabin and put on her swim suit and go swimming. Her broad mouth slipped into a smile and she felt happier than she had in a long time. And to think how close she had come to refusing the beach house, the comfortable and isolated house that seemed to float on its stilts and at night seemed a part of the restless surge of the ocean so near was the sound of the surf.

She had almost passed all of this by, the velvet-soft air, the fishy salt scent of the sea, and, best of all, the freedom. She hadn't felt free in a long time.

Her grip on the charcoal pencil slackened and her hand rested in her lap. She looked past the manila pad but she didn't focus on the gleaming *Sue Belle* or the bright blue water. She was remembering the hot day, unseasonably hot for early May, and the quick patter of heels coming up behind her on the sidewalk outside Brannigan Hall.

"Oh Lee, wait for me."

She waited. It is a little difficult for a tall rangy blonde to do anything else when spotted on a broad flat sidewalk. She turned to face Mary Margaret. With admirable discipline, she managed a smile.

"I'm so glad I saw you." The small plump woman skittered to a stop and seemed, to Lee, to hover with the same quivering eagerness a hummingbird exhibits near a choice flower. Lee stood a little more stiffly.

Mary Margaret pointed at the papers tucked under one arm. "Bluebooks," she exclaimed.

And what, Lee wondered, did she expect to find under the arm of an instructor during finals week: An original Cezanne? Or perhaps a blood-red ruby wrenched from the forehead of an idol secreted deep in an exotic jungle?

"Bluebooks." Mary Margaret repeated. "I'll bet you've just given your last final.

Lee nodded warily. Did Mary Margaret want her to oversee somebody else's final? A final scheduled two weeks from now at midnight in the basement of the stadium?

Mary Margaret slipped her arm through Lee's free arm and continued chattily, "I'll bet you're all hot and tired and on your way to the Union for a beer."

She hadn't been, as a matter of fact, but abruptly her mouth yearned for the cool bitter taste of beer.

"I'll walk along with you, if I may," Mary Margaret continued, "In fact, I'll buy us both a beer to celebrate the end of the semester," and she peered sideways hopefully at Lee.

Lee hesitated. What did Mary Margaret want? Then, with an inward shrug, she decided it didn't really matter. She wanted a beer and she was a big girl. All she had to say was no.

Once at the Union and in the dim cool beer cellar, Lee relaxed back into the red leatherette seat of the booth and eyed Mary Margaret curiously.

Mary Margaret drank her beer and for a long moment said

nothing at all. Then, staring down at the gleaming formica-topped table, she asked abruptly, "What are your plans for the summer, Lee?"

Lee took another great swallow of the sharply cold beer but the pleasure seeped away. Damn them, they never let you forget, she thought angrily. "Don't have any," she replied curtly.

The older woman hesitated, then said quietly, "I'm sorry, Lee. I didn't think." She took a breath. "I'll be frank. I'm hoping to ask a favor of you."

Lee looked up in quick surprise and her defensive posture relaxed a little. She was so accustomed to having favors thrust upon her, so unhappily used to everyone attempting to make things easier and in the course of their kindness only reminding her. The novelty of someone approaching her for a favor was very warming.

"What can I do for you?" And Lee knew she wanted to help the little professor who had been kind to her all this long winter.

"It's my beach house on the Gulf," Mary Margaret explained briskly. "I can't go home this summer and I don't want to rent the house by long distance. I don't worry about leaving it vacant in the winter, but summer's another matter entirely. There are so many tourists. I thought perhaps you might enjoy spending the summer at the shore. As my guest, of course. It would be a great help to me." She fell silent and her bright smile slipped away. For an instant, her face quivered infinitesimally. Then she took a deep breath and pulled the smile back in place. "Padre is such a fascinating place, my dear. Buried treasure and birds and the best harpoon fishing in the world."

Lee had fought her own way out of dark and fearful places and she couldn't ignore that instant when Mary Margaret's smiling mask had fallen away. "Why can't you go home this summer?"

Mary Margaret finished her beer, placed the slender fluted

glass precisely on its circular cork pad. Plump fingers turned the glass around and around. She didn't look at Lee. Her voice was steady but thin when she spoke. "I have to have some surgery. It will require absolute quiet for several She lifted her face ye requires some time for healing. And immo-bility." Her set face barred further questions.

Lee understood. Whatever the surgery, the prognosis must be grim. She knew that only the skill of a surgeon and lots of luck would save her sight. Mary Margaret had tenure, but how secure would she be as a blind professor of English? She was a superb teacher but she hadn't published much. If, she lost her eyesight . . .

If it would comfort Mary Margaret for her to go to Padre, wherever that might be, she would go. She had no plans for the summer. Once she had glorious plans. Mike should have been coming home in June. There would have been a June wedding. Unimaginative, perhaps, but when it is to be your own, a June wedding sounds fresh and wonderful. The flaming maelstrom of a Huey crash outside Bamberg, Germany, in October canceled those plans. Canceled everything for Mike. Lee endured the long winter. She taught classes, graded papers, attended faculty functions and everyone had been kind.

There were awkwardly offered reassurances, you're young, it takes time, you'll meet someone else. Often the words caused more pain though she knew people always meant well. She drank the beer and made no attempt at easy optimism, worthless commiseration. She had learned more this winter than she had ever wished to know.

Instead she asked, "Padre? It sounds marvelous, but what is it? And where is it?"

Mary Margaret smiled, an impish lilting smile. "The local CofC would object, but Padre Island is the world's largest sandbar. Padre runs for about a hundred and ten miles along the Texas Coast from Corpus Christi to Port Isabel. It has everything an island should, including buried treasure and a history of cannibalistic Indians and stories of struggling early settlers. There are masses of gulls and terns, egret and ibis, and miles of sandy beaches so firm you can drive your car on them. My beach house is actually on Mustang Island at the northern end of Padre. You can walk to the water and surf, fish. . . ."

Lee settled back against the slick leatherette seat. She could almost smell the sea and suddenly she knew she wanted to go. And she did.

She'd reached Mustang Island the day before, and she loved the tropical flounce of the palms, air softer than a drifting bird feather, and most of all, the solitude. Not that she was alone on a tropical isle. Padre and its northern extension, Mustang, teemed not only with birds but with swimmers, fishermen, treasure seekers, bird watchers, shell collectors, and a good many people who lived there. But she moved among them unnoticed because no one knew her.

She returned to the sketch, firmly grasped the charcoal pencil, and deepened the shading near the pilings. No one knew her and she knew no one. It was a luxury to savor and hoard. Slowly, she was beginning to feel like the Lee who had laughed so lightheartedly the year before. In her own time and in her own way, she was going to survive. Her new surroundings gave her a sense of peace. No one knew her, there were no sympathetic glances, no well-meant comments. Her friends and colleagues offered kindness always, but kindness can remind and distress. Here in a setting completely strange to her, sketching a boat she would never board, she was not Lee Porter whose fiancée had died in Germany. She was nobody. She didn't exist to anyone else. It was like being invisible. It was as warming and healing to her spirit as the silk-soft air and the warmth of the sun and the incredibly shiny blue sky.

She tilted her head to the right, narrowed her eyes, studied the sketch. She felt a spurt of pleasure. The drawing had an air of reality, the hull glistened just as it did in the bright sunshine. She had captured the *Sue Belle*'s aura of pride.

She was finishing the sketch when a Ford pickup turned into the graveled parking area in front of the marina. The truck jolted to a stop and a beautiful young man swung out of the driver's seat and ran lightly toward what she had come to regard as her boat.

He moved like a tennis player. He was shirtless. Ragged denim shorts hung on his hips. Lee watched with delight his supple grace, the sheer animal beauty of magnificent youth. When he jumped onto the deck of the *Sue Belle*, she flipped to a fresh page on her pad and tried a quick impression of him. She judged him to be eighteen or nineteen. His back was to her and she tried to recreate the ripple of muscles under the smooth dark skin as he bent and lifted an obviously heavy coil of rope.

She smudged through one attempt and dropped down the page to try again. Still she could not bring to life the stretched tendons and taut muscles of his effort.

All right, all right, she thought good-naturedly, so she wasn't Michelangelo. She had done okay on the *Sue Belle* and that was good enough for the start of what she now knew was going to be an idyllic summer. The Idyll of Lee Porter. Perhaps everyone ought to spend one summer as an invisible, sun-warmed wraith.

As she closed her sketchbook, the boy walked to the bow. He knelt and began to work with something out of her view. He was unaware of her scrutiny.

She was fascinated by the darkly-handsome face. She reopened her sketchbook. She might not be up to rippling back muscles, but she enjoyed an easy sureness with portraits, the sort of facility possessed by weary faced men at fairs, good but not quite good enough.

His thick mop of curly black hair gleamed like polished ebony. Dark brown eyes bore lashes any girl might envy, but his heavy cheekbones jutted out, saving him from prettiness, giving his face character. His mouth, though mobile and humorous, also looked tough. As he worked, he whistled a little tune through his teeth.

She drew, paused, drew again. When she finished, she nodded in approval. A good likeness. She was stroking in the long curling sideburns when the boy lifted his head and looked directly across the road at her. His big black eyes took in the sketchbook and her hand poised over it, and he understood and immediately flashed a smile that revealed even white teeth and a good deal of charm.

She smiled back, enjoying the temporary rapport. He bent again to his work. She altered the line of the jaw and she was done. She was standing, gathering up her straw boat purse and her sketchbook and pencils, when the high-pitched whistle of the returning ferry sounded. She decided to stop a moment longer and watch the cars and trucks rumble off.

Two campers and a panel truck and a dusty Oldsmobile pulling a motorboat reached the narrow asphalt road. The last car off was a light-tan Chevrolet, noticeable because it carried a red flasher on its roof, spotlights on both doors, and a black-lettered legend on the side, *SHERIFF'S OFFICE, NUECES COUNTY.*

Lee was enchanted to note, as the car drew nearer, that its rugged-faced driver wore a cowboy hat. If she hadn't been so hungry she would have started another sketch, but she hadn't breakfasted yet so she turned to start up the road toward Pete's café. She wasn't consciously paying attention to the sheriff but an artist's eye sees even when not so instructed. What she saw—a heavy sun-reddened face creased in taut unhappy lines—brought her to a stop. She watched with a gathering frown as the car eased to a stop beside the pickup. The sheriff got out of the car slowly, almost as if he were reluctant. He stood and shaded his face against the bright sunshine and looked out at the *Sue Belle* in the marina.

Lee hoped—irrationally, for it could mean nothing to her—that the sheriff's grim face had nothing to do with the beautiful boy.

The sheriff called, "Hey Johnny, your pop on board?"

The black-haired boy looked up. He was shaking his head even as his face split in a wide smile of greeting. "Hi, sheriff. No, he's not here." Then his youthful features reformed into a sincere but clearly unaccustomed gravity. "No, sir. His sister, my Aunt Rita, died last week, and Dad went to the funeral. She lived in Missouri. He's staying over for a couple of days to help her kids straighten out insurance and stuff. Do you want me to have him call you when he gets back?"

The sheriff's big shoulders hunched a little, and he looked down at the water and shook his big head.

"When did your pop leave, Johnny?"

"Let's see," the boy figured out loud. "Today's Saturday. It must have been Tuesday night that they called. He left Wednesday morning."

"So you've had the *Sue Belle* to yourself since then?"

Johnny nodded proudly.

The sheriff stared at him for a moment, then turned and moved heavily to his car and reached in through the window to pick something up from the seat. When he walked back toward the puzzled boy, Lee could see a square of paper in the older man's hand.

The sheriff went to the edge of the dock and leaned out to hand the paper to the boy. "This is a search warrant, Johnny, for the *Sue Belle*."

"Search warrant?" Johnny repeated the words as if they were meaningless.

The sheriff nodded. "I'm sorry about it."

"What are you talking about?" Johnny demanded. He stared down at the paper. "Search warrant? Why that's crazy! Why would you want to search the *Sue Belle*?"

"A tip, Johnny. A tip that there's cocaine hidden aboard. I better tell you right now that you have a right to call a lawyer and that anything you say may be used against you."

Johnny half-smiled. His tense shoulders relaxed. "Cocaine. Hell, sheriff, that's plain crazy-talk. Somebody just got bored and wanted to rile up the sheriff's office. Why, even if somebody was dumb enough to smuggle cocaine, they wouldn't hide it on a charter boat that doesn't go anywhere. What good would it do somebody to hide cocaine on the *Sue Belle*?"

The sheriff shrugged. "I don't know why anybody would do that, Johnny, but I wouldn't have thought you would. I've known you since you were knee-high to a grasshopper and your pop's one of the finest men in South Texas. I've always liked you fine, Johnny." The sheriff's big face wrinkled into a puzzled frown. "Ten years ago I wouldn't have even come out to check the boat. But I gotta tell you, I don't understand anything anymore. I don't know what's happened to life. I been a sheriff for twenty-three years, and you know something, Johnny, a lot of kids today think it's real good to break the law." He stared at the *Sue Belle*. "I made eight arrests last week for possession of cocaine. In one week. They weren't bums, either. Oh, a couple of them were drifters I picked up over on Kelso Point, but one kid was a doctor's son and another was the daughter of a church organist." He took a deep breath "So I'm gonna search the *Sue Belle*, Johnny."

Johnny's face turned a dull red. He blew out a hard spurt of air. Then, unexpectedly, he smiled. "I'm sorry you don't trust anybody anymore, sir. Sure, you search the *Sue Belle*. You won't find any drugs here."

The deck dipped a little as the sheriff's 240 pounds landed solidly. "I reckon I hope not, Johnny."

The sheriff was a methodical man. He started at the bow and worked back.

Lee, still clutching her purse and sketchbook, was frankly absorbed in the scene aboard the *Sue Belle.* She felt sure the sheriff could regain a little of his faith when he finished his task. The beautiful young man was so completely at ease, so sure of his boat's integrity, that Lee knew the search was pointless. She remained where she was. She wanted to see the sheriff's face when he returned to the dock.

The sheriff was hauling out a length of chain from a locker when the stance of his bent body altered.

Lee knew as surely as if he had shouted out his find. "No, oh no," she murmured.

Johnny saw the sheriff's body tense, too. At first the beautiful young face was only touched by a frown. It took a long moment, the moment when he could see what lay beneath the chain, for his face to break apart. His eyes were shocked. His mouth hung slack. He shook his head back and forth wordlessly, as totally confounded as if the sea had begun suddenly to bubble and froth and sink into the sand.

CHAPTER 3

Dan Holloway didn't have work on his mind as he strode rapidly down Twigg Street. He was in a hurry to start his holiday. In only a little while, maybe an hour, he'd pull on a polo shirt and some ragged khaki shorts and drive down to the marina and see who might be free for charter for a couple of days. Maybe five days. Dan had just wrapped up his last duty, a quick courtesy call on an editor of the *Corpus Christi Caller-Times*, and now he was free. Nobody needed, wanted, or expected anything of him for eight days when he was due in Colima.

He passed a park and admired stocky palm trees and the lush pink flowers on oleander shrubs. He had left St. Louis a week ago, driving away from the thick acrid pall of smog enveloping that lovely city on the river plain, driving south and watching the trees grow smaller as if seen through the wrong end of a telescope, driving finally into rolling hills with stunted bois d'arc, driving farther south yet and into rich black-earthed farming country of southeastern Texas, and finally into the sandy soil near the coast with mesquite and oil derricks and huge refineries. He watched the world turn from temperate to subtropical. He would see more startling changes when he drove farther and farther south into Mexico, winding his way finally to the southwest coast and Colima.

But for now the long days of travel were over. He had a whole week free to enjoy the Gulf, a fisherman's paradise with sailfish, marlin, tarpon, pompano, red snapper. He walked slower, relaxing. At this moment he was in a tremendously happy humor. He had always been a fishing fool. At one point his parents had worried they had bred a water bum, but he had surprised them agreeably with a superb academic record, although archeology was not what his businessman-father termed a solid career. They had been pleased and relieved when, upon completion of his doctorate, he found a job as an assistant curator at the Ward-Stockton Museum.

On his way south, he spent several days in Joplin with his now-widowed mother, trying to bridge the gap of years and interests.

"This trip to Colima, what is it you are going to do?"

Dan stretched his long legs in the white porch swing and gave a leisurely push on the porch railing with his foot. The creak of the metal supports reminded him of years and years of summers in the lush green heat of Missouri. One way of life. He would travel hundreds of miles to probe another way of life that pulsed with energy two thousand years ago.

"It's an excavation, Mother. A whole new series of underground tombs have been located and they are unspoiled. It's a magnificent opportunity."

Her elderly, freckled face brightened. "Do you expect to find treasure?"

He pulled his pipe from his shirt pocket and took his time dipping it into his tobacco pouch. He knew his mother associated tomb exploration with the fabled excavation of King Tutankhamen's royal tomb in Egypt's Valley of the Kings. That sort of archeology she could appreciate.

He filled his pipe, lit it. “Not gold. These are the tombs of a simple village people. These particular people, from the samples found to date, lived around 100 to 300 A.D. Mostly we find burial offerings of clay figurines and pottery vessels.” He leaned forward. “It’s very exciting when we find the figurines. We gain [illegible] most incredibly intimate view of how the people lived, how they danced and what they wore and what kinds of instruments the musicians played.” He broke off at the slight frown on his mother’s face.

She started to speak then changed her mind. For a moment, there was the silence of a summer afternoon with the thick chorus of the cicadas whirring in the trees. Finally she asked hopefully, “Will there be any lady archeologists at Colima?”

He sucked on his pipe and smiled a little. “Just one,” he answered mildly. “She’s married to Dr. Ridley.”

“Oh.”

He remembered, as he swung down the street in Corpus Christi, the world of disappointment reflected in that small monosyllable. He understood her feelings. Most of her friends had grandchildren, as she mentioned often in her letters. She had no little Johnny or Susie to come and spend a part of the summer with Grandma.

Marriage had not come his way. He and Lil had come close but it didn’t work out. There were plenty of pretty girls and it would only tie a man down if he married.

Dan turned right onto Chaparral. There was always Chrissa at the museum. A small frown creased his face. Chrissa—plump, black-haired, accommodating Chrissa—was beginning to take altogether too proprietary an interest in him. He’d better not drop her a postcard, after all.

Ahead of him, a well-formed rear, nicely-presented under a tight red miniskirt, flipped out the doorway of a five-and-dime and swayed up the street. Nice, he judged. Nice right the way down those shapely legs

Dan slowed a little to enjoy the view. She stopped for a red light and he came up beside her. She was pretty, about seventeen or eighteen. Now she was voluptuous. She would probably be a fat thirty. His mildly-lewd interest swept his eyes past the pretty face to the braless breasts fully-rounded beneath a tight white jersey.

His breath constricted in his chest as violently as if a jackboot had caught him full in the ribs.

She heard his involuntary gasp and half-turned. She looked up at his face, saw his gaze locked on her chest, and her hand jerked up to cover the ornament. But he had seen the incredible piece of jewelry and he would never forget the image, the bright sheen of gold, the delicate scrollwork encompassing the solid central figure of Equetzalcoatl, the god of wind, of life, and of morning, the god of Venus, the god of abundance, the saintly benevolent benefactor of his people, worshipped by the Huastecs, the Toltecs, the Aztecs.

Shown the piece in a museum or in the midst of a scholarly gathering, he would disclaim authority. Aztec metalwork was not his field. He was much more familiar with the massive somber stonework of the Toltecs. But no matter the incongruity, the absurdity of glimpsing the work in this fashion, he knew the piece was genuine and priceless. Nothing would persuade him otherwise.

The glimpse and the swift movement of her covering hand happened so quickly that only later would he wonder why he hadn't grabbed her on the spot, demanded to know where she got the piece and how. But he was a civilized man. Many habits are ingrained. You do not walk about without your trousers. You do not blow your nose on your sleeve. You do not grab young women in public places and shout at them.

For a frozen instant, he and the girl stared at each other. Dan saw the plump dark-skinned hand clasped over her breast, wide staring dark eyes, a rounded cheeky face. Her lips began to tremble.

She gave him a scared, hunted look and whirled away, darting into the street. Her hand pulled at her blouse. A pickup truck slid to the right as the driver stamped on the brake to avoid hitting her. His horn blared. The girl reached the middle of the street and jolted to a stop, blocked by a lumbering bus.

Dan ran after her. Abruptly the morning was alive with noise. Horns shrilled and hooted and blasted. Dan was beside her and reaching out.

She put up both hands to ward him off.

The bus driver yelled down from above them, "Hey, lady, is that man bothering you?"

She looked up and Dan saw indecision in her face.

"Don't be scared," he said loudly, "I only want to ask you some questions."

"Get out of the street," shouted the driver of a truck behind the bus.

Horns yelped like frenzied dogs, then fell silent as the light changed and traffic surged. Other pedestrians were in the lane. The girl moved quickly ahead.

Dan hurried after her. She reached the curb and slipped into the center of the people waiting to cross. He stood, tall enough to look down on her and close enough to reach out and grab her, but she was as effectively beyond his grasp as if she traveled in the midst of an armed guard. He saw curious sidelong glances angled toward him by some of those waiting. A pimply-faced teenager with shoulder-length hair snickered.

Dan's angular face hardened. He thrust his head forward. He

could see those full-blown curves and the taut-stretched white jersey with no distracting glitter. She'd taken the pin off. His eyes dropped to the fringed shoulder bag that hung from her left shoulder. Her left hand gripped the clasp so tightly that the honey-brown hand splotched white.

If he grabbed the purse . . . He was amused at his instinctive recoil from the thought. A social anthropologist would obtain an unholy amount of glee from Dan's emotional responses to the last few minutes. But aside from his somewhat surprising moral hang-up against purse snatching, public theft would be stupid and in the long run a dead end.

He wanted to know more than the object could tell him. He already knew much from his brief glance. The piece was real. The golden god was quite likely Aztec art of the *cire perdue* process where wax is molded, covered with clay, and fired. The wax runs out and the mold is filled with molten gold. The ornament was of incalculable value. So far as he knew nothing quite like it had survived anywhere. There was no legitimate way the piece could be in the possession of the frightened girl standing so near him.

The street light flashed green and the girl walked fast, shoulders hunched.

Dan lowered his head with the obdurate look his handball partner would have recognized and shouldered his way past two plump matrons He caught his quarry at the opposite curb and grabbed her left elbow.

"Let go of me."

"Listen to me and listen hard. You can't talk your way past that pin. Ten'll get you one you've got a safety pin taped to the back to make it stay on. The dumbest cop will see there's something different about it. I'll yell 'stolen goods' so loud they'll at least give you the once-over because there's no way it can belong to you." Her soft plump arm trembled beneath his hand. Automatically, he loosened his hold. His eyebrows bunched in concern when he looked in her eyes. Huge and young, the brown eyes widened in panic. Tears brimmed.

He was shaken. She was just a kid. All that body and just a kid. "Wait a minute," he said gently. "Don't be scared. I don't want to scare you. I just want to talk to you."

Tears brimmed and trickled down her cheeks, scoring through her powder base. She lifted one hand to wipe across her eyes. Bright purple eye shadow mingled with the peach tone of powder.

He continued quietly, "I just need to know where that pin came from."

She opened that absurdly-painted mouth, closed it, opened it again like a beached fish. She gasped, "I'll put it back. I promise. I didn't mean to take it, but it was so pretty and I didn't think one little piece would matter. The color is so shiny, like gold. Please don't tell the police. If the police come, Mrs. Bailey will put me out because she has to keep her place respectable and she says that I wear too much makeup and eye shadow and everything. If she puts me out, I don't have anywhere to go." The tears flooded and she made little choking hiccupping sounds.

"I won't call the police. You don't have to cry. Everything's going to be all right."

"And what would you be wanting with the girl, mister?" a tough voice demanded.

Dan looked up into the face of a broad-shouldered, burly cop who stared with cold eyes. Dan looked past him at a squad car at the curb with its open door and another watchful cop in the driver's seat.

The cop shoved his cap to the back of his head and bent down to the girl. He asked very quietly, "Is this man bothering you, little lady?"

Oh God, Dan thought. They'd run him in for molesting children in another minute. "Look," Dan began, but the cop's hand chopped down. He wasn't interested in what the nasty old man had to say. He wanted to listen to the little lady.

The girl clutched her fringed purse to her chest and looked from the cop to Dan.

Dan understood her dilemma. She didn't dare accuse Dan because he might turn her in for theft but she couldn't make a fool out of the policeman.

Her face crumpled and she began to sob in earnest. "I want to go home. Please, I just want to go home. Just let me go home."

The policeman nodded and patted her shoulder. "That's okay, little girl. You can go in a minute but first, did this man bother you?"

The word 'bother' held an ugly implication.

CHAPTER 4

Every fifth breaker loomed higher than its fellows. They were small beer compared to California combers, but often enough one boomed in that was big enough to dive under or to turn and ride in to shore. Warm sudsy water flowed around Lee's waist as she watched the incoming waves, waiting for a big one. When a good one came, she dived into the wall of water. The powerful sweep of the wave surged the length of her—and it wasn't any damn fun.

She came up, swam a stroke or two, abruptly stood. She turned and sloshed toward the beach. She had looked forward to this swim. Her morning had been so well-programmed, an early outing with her sketchbook, a leisurely breakfast, the unhurried drive home to the beach house, then finally, in the warmth of midmorning, a climb down the weathered wooden steps and a quick walk across sand to the water.

She had done all of these things, but the shine of the morning was gone. That stricken young face obtruded, that beautiful face emptied and slack. She had never before seen confidence in life, in reason, in ordered existence abruptly and cruelly destroyed.

She moved, long-limbed and graceful, into the rippling shallows then onto hard-packed wet sand, polished clean by the in-and-out surge of the sea. Just past the stretching fan of the sea water, she picked up her beach towel and slipped on thongs.

The beach stretched as far as the eye could see in either direction. A few red-and-orange striped umbrellas sprouted like oversized mushrooms. A child dug with a plastic spade and watched with the same fascinated eye as that little boy of long ago who watched the sea come up 'til it could come no more. A high school boy, his thick golden curls soft against his damp curling beard, leaned over his girl to kiss softly, so softly, the hollow of her throat. A thirtyish mother in a too-tight bikini, hips just a little too plump, legs just a little too flabby, rubbed suntan lotion on the back of a squirming sandy-haired boy, warning, "Hold still, Bobby. No, see what you did. You kicked sand in the basket. I hope you like sandy peanut butter and jelly sandwiches." The little boy wormed free. Her voice rose. "Wait, your nose." Then she looked out at the water and came up from the blanket in a wild, ungainly surge. "Susie, you come back here this minute. Not out past the third wave! Susie, do you hear. . . ."

Lee gently shook out her towel, shedding sticky grains of sand. She looked up and down the beach. There were just enough people to be cheerful. It was almost deserted by resort beach standards. Then, decisively, she folded the towel. She couldn't stretch and turn in the sun, run and splash in the soft Gulf water as if she had never seen a boy's world crumble around him.

Her decisiveness lasted all the way through her shower. She soaped briskly, washing away suntan oil and a sticky film of salt and grains of sand that clung like filings to a magnet. She stepped out onto the lilac-colored bath mat, toweled quickly, hurried into the combination living and bedroom. She slipped into panties and bra, a pale blue blouse and short white skirt. She twisted her thick blonde hair back and tied a blue scarf in a small cheerful bow. She buckled on her white sandals, picked up her straw purse, then paused uncertainly in the middle of the Navajo rug.

All dressed up and no place to go. What, after all, could she do to restructure the handsome boy's world? And why, with all her delight in her freedom and anonymity, should she feel compelled to meddle in someone else's life?

But the boy's father was somewhere in Missouri. So? This was Johnny's hometown. Surely he had a mother and brothers, perhaps uncles and cousins, someone to take care of him. She didn't know that, however. She frowned. Good grief, he wasn't her responsibility, her charge. Her anything.

He was so young.

She turned and crossed to the door, uncomfortably aware that she was very likely going to make a fool of herself. Well, it wouldn't do any harm to go to the marina. Perhaps, even now, he was back aboard the *Sue Belle*.

The VW skittered like a jaunty ladybug into the dockside parking. Lee nudged the bumper of the little car right up to the stone retaining wall and stared across the few feet at the deserted deck and cabin of the *Sue Belle*. She looked around the marina. There were other untenanted boats moving slowly up and down in the water. But somehow the *Sue Belle* seemed ominously still. That was only, of course, because of the scene she had witnessed earlier that morning. Her eyes roved to the locker where the sheriff had stiffened like a good dog on point. The varnished deck glistened in the midday sunshine. All of the *Sue Belle* seemed to glisten.

Where was the boy now? In the dimness of a concrete-block jail cell?

She got out of the VW and walked to the wall. It didn't do any good to stare at the *Sue Belle*. He wasn't there. No one was there. She turned and looked toward the main street of the little village. Her gaze fastened on the shining metal siding of an outdoor phone booth. She hurried to the booth and pulled out the squeaky door. She flipped open the thin blue phone book, traced her finger down a page, slowly closed the book. What would she ask when the sheriff's office answere[illegible] She didn't even know Johnny's last name. Which proved that if you knew as little about someone as she did of the boy, you didn't have any business meddling. She dropped the phone book and it dangled limply from the metal linked chain.

That was that. It was an unhappy interlude, something that she would have wished not to witness, such as a bad car smash or a bitter exchange between a husband and wife, but it wasn't her life that had been altered. Now it was time to pick up the shining thread of her summer, time to savor again that strange ghostlike freedom.

She stepped out of the phone booth and walked up the black-topped road with a certain finality, concentrated on the scene here and now.

She crossed Cotter to climb wide wooden steps to a white-painted verandah shared by several shops. She walked slowly along the verandah, pausing at each shop to look at the window display. Cheerful yellow fishnet provided the background for a red-and-white striped jersey blouse and bright red Capri pants in The Casual Corner. Next door, sunglasses, suntan lotions, cameras, ice buckets, and flashlights cluttered the small display case of The Notions Shop. She moved past that window with scarcely a pause, then stood entranced at the last shop.

Unlike the other stores along the veranda with their broad plate-glass fronts, this shop had a multi-paned front. Through each pane, she could see a single exhibit as if framed by the glistening white wood.

A gleaming brass warming pan, its turned wooden handle

rubbed soft with age, shone through one pane. A Betty lamp hung in the center of another. A vivid Tiffany vase sat on a drop-leaf table. Framed in the bottom right-hand pane was a book, its faded green binding crumbling around the edges. Lee leaned down to read *A Partial History, Annotated, of San Patricio County, From Earliest Times*, by Gerald Henry Wilson.

It was an antique shop, of course, but one unlike any other Lee had ever chanced upon. In the left-hand corner window, neat black letters proclaimed OF THINGS PAST. Smaller printing added, CURIOS, MOMENTOES, MEMORABLIA, COPIES. Small gilt letters informed, *PROP. E. ABBOTT.*

Lee might have passed by but for the small green book. She didn't have a consuming interest in the people and the passions that had worked upon the history of San Patricio County, but she was a sucker for old books. And there, not more than five feet past the door, was a table covered with all sorts and shapes of old books. A neat sign, hand printed this time, informed OLD BOOKS OF MODERATE VALUE.

She was inside the shop before she even consciously made a decision.

It was always like coming home when she found books and gently opened the covers to their title pages. There is a special magic about old books, dusty tattered survivors of another day. To Lee, they always reemphasized the continuity of human experience and, at the same time, gently reminded how temporal the influence of even the most popular and instructive of works.

She picked up first one then another, a life of Thomas Jefferson written in the 1880's, its language ponderous and self-important; a highly technical exposition of Marconi's recent experiments, published in 1914, and an early copy of *The Guardian Angel* by Oliver Wendell Holmes. She looked them over and then she saw a small stack of yellowing pamphlets.

She held seven small magazines each about nine inches long and six inches wide. They were printed on medium-weight once-white paper. Seven copies of *The Editor, The Journal of Information for Literary Workers.* The top one in the stack had been published December 30, 1916. It was No. 14 of Vol.44. The contents were listed on the cover and Lee smiled as she read "The Essence of Realism," "Imaginative Treatment," "The Photoplay Plot," "The Proper Time to Take Photos," and on and on. Price—ten cents a copy. Lee turned the small pages and saw ads of books and magazines for beginning writers. She wondered if somewhere in the world any one of these books survived, moldering in an attic or basement. She would particularly love to have a copy of Writing for Vaudeville by Brett Page. According to the ad, the contents would help the reader to write the monologue, two-act playlets, musical comedy, the popular song, and so on. It ran 650 pages and sold for $2.15.

Lee held the journals firmly in her hand and looked around for E. Abbott, Prop. The room was wide and deep and on all sides Lee saw things of interest. A huge section to her left offered copies of pre-Columbian Mexican art and one shelf of genuine artifacts. Along the wall to her right ran a waist-high shelf filled with dioramas.

Lee veered from the center aisles and walked slowly alongside the shelf with the dioramas. Washington crossed the Delaware and white froth topped the choppy waves and droplets of ice glittered on the gunwale. St. Paul walked along the road to Damascus and the tiny figure had a stalwart aura as he strode on the rutted desert pathway. Santa Ana's troops clambered up the breach in the Alamo, trampling underfoot the bodies of those who had resisted to the last.

With an artist's eye, Lee studied the meticulous work, the careful attention to scale, the authenticity of the modeled figures, and the bright sheen of the painted backgrounds. She judged that all the dioramas had been made by the same person, and she marveled at the catholic world-ranging interests the artist possessed, from Damascus to San Antonio, from the Appian Way to the Great Wall.

A neatly typewritten card entitled and described each diorama. Lee bent close. Yes, in each corner it read *ARTIST E. ABBOTT*. SO *PROP., E. ABBOTT*; *ARTIST, E. ABBOTT*. Lee wanted to meet E. Abbott.

There was one final diorama set a bit apart. The card read, *D-DAY, 6 JUNE 1944, JUNO BEACH, NOT FOR SALE.*

Lee looked back up the row. Most of them were priced at $200, which was quite reasonable considering the time and grace involved in each creation. Why was this last one not for sale? It had certainly not been the most difficult to execute. She looked back up the row. The hardest must have been *Hiram Bingham discovering Machu Picchu*. In comparison, Juno Beach was an exercise in simplicity. Lee shrugged. One could scarcely have a sentimental . . . She pulled away from the inevitable understanding. At least she had thought before she asked.

She turned away from the displays, moving toward the center aisle, and for a moment the savor was gone.

Juno Beach, Bamberg. She could think of both places at once, bring them together in her mind, but for some the last finite instant of awareness had been bound by the actual physical dimensions of. . . .

"May I help you?"

Lee came back from a long distance. She held up her handful of journals. "I wondered how much you wanted for these?"

"Seventy-five cents each," The woman smiled. "They're fun, aren't they?" she asked, almost shyly. "If you like this sort of thing, I'll show you something I bought last week." She led the way toward the front of the shop. “It isn’t for sale yet. I need to repair the album cover.”

At the display case behind the front windows, she knelt and opened a cupboard and gently lifted out a thick ledger-sized album and rested it on the counter. She opened the worn volume carefully and Lee could see the issue of January 2, 1896 of *The Youth’s Companion*, the illustrated weekly paper for young people. The volume held a full year’s subscription.

The year of 1896 started off with a bang. The first issue featured the beginning serialization of a high adventure novel, *The Clutch of the Tsar*. Lee read the first few paragraphs. As she carefully turned brittle pages, she noted ads for Beeman’s Gum and Harvard University and Phoenix bicycles. The second chapter of the serial ran in the January 9 issue. In the drop head, the upcoming action was outlined: TAKEN TO THE TOWN JAIL.—ROBBED BY THE SOLDIERS.—THRUST INTO BAD COMPANY, A DINGY COURT-ROOM AND A SEVERE SENTENCE,—PUT WITH A CHAIN GANG—AT A COAL-MINE.—ITS TERRORS, AN UNPLEASANT ENCOUNTER.

“It’s wonderful.”

The small, soft-spoken shopkeeper smiled at Lee’s pleasure. “It’s the sort of buy that keeps you going to estate sales. I bought two crates of old books. Most of them were not of much interest but in the bottom of the second crate I found this and—” She broke off abruptly.

Lee looked up to see why.

The older woman stood, half turned toward the window. She gazed at the two police cars parked by the sea wall and at uniformed men, four of them, who were boarding the *Sue Belle*.

CHAPTER 5

Sweat beaded on Dan's face and trickled into his sideburns and mustache until his whole face was hot and itchy. The air was stale and hot in the back seat of the police car. He finally gave up trying to explain as the officer in the driver's seat ignored him.

Dan wiped the back of his hand across his face. He hadn't sweated like this since he'd worked on a wheat farm one summer. He wondered what convicts did in Texas—pick cotton, make license plates, or dig ditches?

Outside the car, the big tough-faced cop spoke quietly to the girl who stood by the squad car, crying. The cop's conviction that Dan was an incipient rapist was clear in his gentle concern for the girl and continued rebuff of Dan.

"How about we go along to the station and you can call someone to come and get you?"

The girl sobbed harder at that so they stood next to the car and the cop tried to get her story. "Now, little lady, you just tell us what happened. We won't let him bother you anymore. But we have to know what he did."

"I wanted to talk to her." Dan tried to hold on to his temper.

"Shut up."

The girl finally borrowed a handkerchief and scrubbed at her face then looked at her watch. "Please," her voice was frantic, "I have to go. I have to be back before lunch. Please, I have to go."

The big policeman frowned. "If this man scared you, we need to know about it."

The girl shot a scared look at Dan. "He didn't do anything bad. I misunderstood." Her eyes pled with Dan. "I got to go now."

"Okay." The cop's tone was grudging. "Where do you live, little lady?"

"Aransas Pass," the girl said in a small voice.

"How're you going to get home?" the policeman asked.

"The bus. If I hurry, I can catch the next one."

"All right, miss. If you're sure this man didn't bother you."

She shook her head quickly, her eyes wide and dark.

The policeman slowly nodded.

Dan began to breathe a little easier.

The policeman said gruffly, "All right then, you get along home."

The girl turned and walked away, hurrying shoulders bent.

The policeman turned back into the car, and his face was hard and ugly when he looked at Dan. "Now listen, you sonofabitch, you stop chasing ass in my town or you're gonna get yourself in jail so fast you won't believe it." The cop yanked open the door to the back seat. He gestured—a sharp, vicious jab with his thumb. "Get out of here. I'm telling you, buddy, we don't like your kind. And when we don't like somebody, it takes that elevator a long time to get from the booking floor to the cell floor."

Dan climbed out of the back seat, knew he looked hot, sweaty, and red-faced. "I wasn't trying to pick up that girl."

"Can it," the cop interrupted. "Give me your driver's license."

Dan's head had swung left and he watched that plump mini-skirted rear hurry across the street. On the corner was a bus station.

"My driver's license?" he repeated. He looked at the policeman and frowned irritably 'What for? I'm not driving."

"You're a real smart guy, aren't you?" the cop rejoined. "I thought you had your card right here in the back seat with you. But that's all right, mister, you don't have to show it to me. We'll just take a little drive down to the station and I'll ask you again."

Dan glared at him. "Wait a minute. I'm not breaking any law. You don't have any right to harass me."

The cop was pulling the squad car door open again. "If you don't have any identification, mister, you're a vagrant so we'll go to the station."

Dan risked another quick look. The girl was walking into the bus station. He faced the policeman again, pulled his billfold out of his pocket, "I misunderstood you, officer," he said quietly. "I do, of course, have identification. If you would like to check further, an old friend of mine works for the newspaper and I have some colleagues on the staff at Del Mar." He had the license out now and was handing it to the policeman. "I'd like to assure you that this has been a total misunderstanding. The young lady has some information I would like to have. It doesn't concern her personally."

The policeman read the license over carefully then looked steadily at Dan. Gradually, the hard lines in his face eased a little. He was not totally convinced. It doesn't take too many years for a cop to learn that the most respectable of manners can mask great evil. But he had no real handle on Dan and he saw, now that he looked carefully, that here was someone who might have a good deal of stroke despite his overlong hair and thick mustache and sideburns.

He handed back the license. "You can go. But don't let me see you with your hands on any more girls."

Tightlipped, Dan gave a short nod. He stood on the sidewalk and put his license back in his billfold and watched the squad car slowly pull away. He turned and walked back the way he had come. Even at the risk of losing the girl, he didn't dare cross the street and go directly to the bus station. If that cop saw him near her again, he'd be at the station in a heartbeat. He had no interest in finding out just how long it could take that jail elevator to move between floors.

She said she was going home, home to Aransas Pass. It was a small town on the mainland not far from the ferry crossing to Port Aransas on Mustang Island.

He walked up the street, all the while aching to turn and run to the terminal and confront her. He looked down at his watch. Ten-eighteen. How soon would the next bus leave for Aransas Pass?

His MG was parked at a meter behind the *Caller-Times* building. He calculated the distance. Three and a half blocks. He could reach it in a couple of minutes and it was within a half-block of the freeway that the bus would travel. He didn't dare return to the bus station. Instead, he'd drive to Aransas Pass and await the bus.

What if she lied? What if she didn't live in Aransas Pass? He hurried on up the street. If he was wrong about her, he was going to lose touch with something of incalculable value. But he thought she was telling the truth. He thought, though it was a little incongruous, that she was an honest person. She had somehow managed to heist a piece that would go at auction for a cool half-million, but still he thought she was honest. So he was going to Aransas Pass.

The MG surged onto the freeway. The car was a delight to drive. Preoccupied though he was, he still savored the rush of wind when the MG topped the rise of the Harbor Bridge and swooped down the other side. The bridge emptied onto the broad Nueces Bay Causeway that ran flat and straight across mud flats then swung inland for a while past fields of broom corn and stands of irregular palms and the bright poetry of hibiscus.

Just short of Aransas Pass, he eased the MG onto the shoulder and into the shade of an oleander shrub. He leaned back against the red leather seat to await the rumble of the bus. He slowly filled and tamped his pipe. As he smoked, his eyes squinted in thought.

Where had that incredible piece of gold come from? Could there possibly have been a museum theft of which he was unaware? Since that was his world, his life, it seemed unlikely. Moreover, though he would disclaim with a scholar's quick modesty any exhaustive mental catalog of Mexican artifacts, he was, he thought, acquainted with the most magnificent finds. That delicate golden rendering of Quetzalcoatl would be a treasure in anybody's museum.

He puffed slowly on his pipe. His thick reddish eyebrows hunkered in a frown. Was he mistaken? That timeless instant when he had stared at the golden ornament was clear in his mind. The memory of the golden god was sharp and distinct. The gold was a special gold. It did not have the hard metallic glitter of modern gold, but the particular soft glisten of old hand-worked metal. True enough, the god's form appeared to be molded, but the goldsmith had been an artist. He had taken his solid core of gold, elaborate though it was with a headdress and masked face, breast-piece and ankle bracelets, and welded to it a most delicate filigree of worked gold. The whole gave an effect of total individuality and grace and integrated design that no modern work could possibly equal or imitate. The piece was not a forgery, not a hoax.

He chewed on the stem of his pipe. It ruined his pipes too soon but he had done it for years when baffled. He chewed and listened again in his mind to the breathless tumbling words of the girl. They didn't make any more sense now than they had at the time. How could anyone possibly not know the worth of that ornament? She said she didn't think "one little piece would matter." That implied there were more pieces, didn't it? More pieces? His chest felt tight and his pulse thrummed in his ears.

He moved uneasily in the seat. The MG didn't really have enough leg room for him, beautifully though she might sweep down the road. Suddenly, his collar was tight. He yanked at it with his left hand. More pieces?

He looked back up the road. Where the devil was the bus? How long had he been here? Fifteen minutes? Twenty? Too long, but he couldn't have missed the bus. What if it came another way? What way, he couldn't imagine because this was the main road, the traveled road. Even the thought that he might have lost his tenuous contact with the brooch brought his hand to the ignition. The motor growled to life. The MG hummed with power but he remained at the side of the road because there was no better place to go. Sweat trickled down his face.

Twice a heavy rumble brought his hand to the stick shift. Twice his shoulders slumped. Oil trucks.

Finally a red-and-white bus lumbered into view.

The bus passed and the MG eased onto the road like a cat gliding over short grass in pursuit of an unwary bird. He followed the exhaust-spewing bus into the city limits of Aransas Pass. The bus rumbled down the sort of street that leads through every little town in the south and west, one- and two-story business buildings, a drugstore, bakery, coin laundry, shoe store, super market, department store. The bus pulled into a small station. He drove past, found a parking spot.

He had no difficulty following her from the station. She walked two blocks quickly, passing a used clothing store, a barber shop, a five-and-dime. She ducked around one side of a small café at the front of a modest motel converted to apartments. The *N* in Nightingale Courts had slipped a little to the right. Made of faded pink stucco, the color was more a hint of pink than a bright wash of color. Dan turned into the parking lot and drove up beside her. The car was between the girl and the doors to the units.

She heard the throaty growl of the motor and turned to look. She saw him and her lips parted. She looked around in a panic, then hurried to the open car window. "Don't follow me. Bailey will see you. I'll put it back, I promise."

For all that he wanted more than anything to touch that piece of gold and know its story, he couldn't ignore the anguish in her cry.

She looked back toward the café, then stepped closer to the car. "Pretend I'm giving you directions. If anyone ever asks, I'll tell them you pulled in to get directions." She pointed back up toward the street,

Dan nodded and pretended to gaze behind him, but his words were crisp. "I have to talk to you. I don't give a damn about your putting it back. I want to know where it came from."

The girl looked surprised. The stress eased from her face. "It didn't come from anywhere," she said blankly.

He was turning to glare at her when she waggled her hand toward the street. He obediently swiveled his face away.

"Where do you live?" he asked sharply. "Can I come and talk to you."

"No." She was abruptly frightened again.

He kept his voice pleasant. "Can I meet you downtown somewhere?"

"Oh, there's Mrs. Bailey." She stared at a heavyset woman standing outside the café, a hand shading her eyes from the sun, her face turned toward the car.

"I have to hurry. I'm late," the girl said. "Look mister, where do you live?"

He frowned. "I'm on my way to Mustang. I usually stay at La Casa Hermosa."

She nodded energetically. "I know that place, mister. Look, I'll meet you at the end of the boardwalk tonight. At nine o'clock. Now, please go."

The elderly woman began to walk toward the car.

Dan looked at the girl's nervous face. "Thanks for the directions," he called out loudly, loudly enough for the old lady to hear. He swung the MG around and headed for the street, his right turn light signaling. Nine o'clock. At the end of the boardwalk.

CHAPTER 6

The sheriff's badge was a gold star. The star had little round balls on the tip of each point. Lee unobtrusively glanced down by the side of the shabby desk at a gleaming brass spittoon. The sheriff would have looked at home in a Walt Disney movie except that his heavy florid face was not the least vacuous and his gray eyes were alert and somber.

He leaned against the front of his desk and the tip end of his holster touched the scarred desktop. "I'm sorry, Evelyn, but I can't let him go. He's been charged with possession of cocaine." He frowned. "Now Evelyn, don't you look at me like that. I found the cocaine, I had to bring him in."

"He told you he didn't put it there," the small sandy-haired woman rejoined quickly.

A smile flickered on the sheriff's face "What would you expect him to say?"

"Sheriff," Lee said quietly, and they both turned to look at her with some surprise. In a sense, she surprised herself. What was she doing here, championing a boy she didn't know? The shopkeeper was a former teacher. She knew the boy. When Lee asked about him and the *Sue Belle*, the owner was eager for Lee to offer her testimony to the sheriff. Not that it apparently was going to help the boy. But she was here and she knew what she had seen and she was going to make her claim again. "As I told you, Sheriff, I was watching this morning when you searched the *Sue Belle*. When you found that package, I saw Johnny's face. He had no idea the drugs were hidden there. I am absolutely certain."

"He could have been shocked that I found them."

Lee shook her head decisively, "There is a difference between shock at being caught and incredulous disbelief at the result of a search."

The sheriff shrugged his heavy shoulders. "Maybe, maybe not. I got a tip. I found cocaine. I made an arrest," The phone rang. He grabbed the receiver. "Sheriff Costello." He listened, his face still, his eyes intent. "You're sure?" he asked quietly. Then he nodded slowly "That is unusual, Paul. We almost always find a lot when it's packed like that." His weathered face furrowed in well-worn creases "Yeah. Could be it was a one-shot deal and he was treading on somebody else's territory." He listened again then agreed "Right. It doesn't matter as long as we found all of it. Close it up and come on in."

He hung up the phone, looked at the two women. "The men you saw boarding the *Sue Belle* have finished their search." He paused. "They didn't find any more cocaine. Or anything else." He walked around behind his desk and sat down. "And that's peculiar."

"Peculiar?" Lee asked.

He nodded his big head slowly. He looked at Lee and said very politely. "You see, Miss Porter, you being a teacher, you wouldn't know too much about dope and how pushers get it, how it's shipped."

Lee was tempted to point out that teachers knew almost more about cocaine than a lot of pushers, but she remained quiet.

The sheriff was explaining. "When you read in the paper

that somebody's been picked up and charged with possession of cocaine, usually it means the police found a little baggie of cocaine in a car or pocket or purse." He leaned back his chair and his heavy, muscular body dwarfed the metal curves of the state-issued furniture. He looked big and abruptly tough, "Now that's what we find when we pick up kids who are messin' around with drugs. We don't find kilo-weight hard-packed blocks of cocaine." He shook his head slowly. "When we find a solid block, we've caught a dealer." He looked at the sandy-haired older woman. "That's what I found on the *Sue Belle*, Evely

Impatience flickered in Evelyn Abbott's faded blue eyes but she spoke quietly. "I taught for twenty-nine years, Howard. I learned a good deal about boys and girls in that time. I had Johnny in class for two years, in geometry and intermediate algebra. Johnny is good at math. He's very careful, very thorough." She looked down for a moment, smoothing the pleats in her navy-blue linen skirt. She spoke, almost as if to herself. "You learn so much about your boys and girls. You find out who's greedy and who's kind, who's dour and who's positive. You learn to know the cheats, the liars, the gamblers." She looked up at the sheriff. "Day after day they come to your class. You know them, Howard. You learn the temper of their minds. Johnny is an interesting boy. Things have always come easily to him—school, girls, good times. It's been easy in part because he is so attractive and in part because he is so alive and joyous. Everyone likes Johnny. If he has had any difficulty, it is his remarkable good looks. He has always felt constrained to prove his toughness, his masculinity. If you came to me and said that Johnny had smoked pot with a gang of his friends, I could believe it. He wouldn't care to be made fun of, to be the one who wouldn't. I can see him in that kind of situation although I frankly would be surprised if you caught him at it. He thinks ahead. He would be much more likely to smoke pot on somebody's boat out in the Gulf where there would be no chance of discovery." She stood and crossed to stand in front of the desk. Small, determined, persuasive. "But to tell me that Johnny Fernandez is a pusher, that he has a kilo of cocaine to sell for a profit—that, I will never believe. Never."

"People get greedy—" the sheriff began.

Miss Abbott nodded. "People do. Not Johnny." She spread her hands wide. "You know this in your heart, Howard. You know Johnny and his father. Why, Tom is an old friend of yours. You grew up with him on the island. You know their pride." She reached across the desk to gently touch the sheriff's hand, "In all the years I've known Johnny, he's never told me how much money they made from a charter trip. He always told me what they caught. The first tarpon of the season, that's what matters to them. They worked hard to earn enough money to buy the new boat. Johnny's so proud of the *Sue Belle* II. He wouldn't do anything to jeopardize that boat."

Miss Abbott walked slowly back to her chair and sat down. "Think about it, Howard," she insisted. "Think about the people you know who want money. Money is all they ever talk about. Something cost this much, they made that much on a deal, they're going to make so much tomorrow. Not the Fernandezes. Johnny always told me what they caught, where they fished, how many steady customers who come back every summer because the *Sue Belle* is such a fine boat."

The sheriff nodded thoughtfully. "I would've reasoned that way myself, Evelyn. But you can't get away from the fact that I found a kilo block of pressed cocaine on the *Sue Belle*. That's professional stuff. Somebody hid that block there and Johnny's been the only one on the boat since his dad left town Wednesday."

"Let's talk to Johnny." Her voice held a plea. "Let's see what he says."

The sheriff lowered his head like a big bull. "I can't. The courts got us so hedged around on what we can do with prisoners that I'm not going to take any chances. They'd say he incriminated himself or that his lawyer should have been present. Fact of the matter, I can't ask him anything myself 'til he has a lawyer. I can't seem to track down Tom. He left Bodine, Missouri, this morning on his way home. Johnny won't call a lawyer or anything 'til his dad gets back so I've arranged for one of the public defenders to come over here Monday so I can ask him some questions myself."

Miss Abbott's gentle mouth tightened.

"Evelyn," the sheriff said quickly, "there's no use you getting upset. If you want to come to visiting hours, that's on Thursdays, you can talk to him."

One of Lee's friends the past year was a counselor at her college so she had more than a passing acquaintance with cocaine charges and what happened between arrest and trial. "Has bail been set?" Again her quiet voice surprised them. They had all but forgotten her presence.

"That's a wonderful idea," Miss Abbott said happily.

The sheriff looked at Lee with narrowed eyes, spoke slowly. "Judge McCracken set bail at $1000."

Lee nodded and looked at Miss Abbott. "That's easy enough to manage. I think the bondsmen charge around $100."

"A bondsman. Why, of course," Miss Abbott agreed. "We can get him out of jail. Do you know, Lee, I hadn't even thought of that."

Lee could see that the sheriff was interested in her familiarity with bail and bondsmen and was discarding his easy characterization of her as a spinster school teacher. And putting in its place Lord knew what.

It took time. All things connected with the law take time. Shortly past noon, they were once again at the county jail. They heard from down a corridor the clang of steel doors and the light tread of tennis shoes and the hard clump of steel-edged leather heels. Johnny came into the lobby of the jail, a deputy sheriff close behind him.

Johnny was half-turned, staring back over his shoulder at the deputy. "Where are you taking me?" His voice was gruff, but the gruffness didn't mask fear.

"Straight ahead," the deputy said indifferently. "Some folks to see you."

Johnny's head jerked around. When he saw the two of them, the small sandy-haired woman and the tall long-legged blonde, his expressive face reflected total surprise. His big dark eyes glowed with hope. He stopped, just inside the door to the small lobby, and looked up at the deputy. "Is everything okay? Can I go home?"

For an instant, a brief instant, compassion flickered in the older man's face. He said kindly enough, "You can go home, son, because they posted bond. You'll be notified when the trial date is set and the district attorney's office will set a time for questions when you have a lawyer."

Johnny's head yanked back as if he'd been slapped. Clearly he'd thought for a moment that the nightmare was over, that somehow everything had been made right, that the law had realized that he hadn't put cocaine on the *Sue Belle*. The deputy's gentle-enough response obviously hit him like a knee in the chest. His face crumpled.

Miss Abbott slipped her arm around his waist and gently steered him toward the door. "Johnny, we'll figure this out. No matter what the problem, there is always a solution."

To the frightened boy, the words must have seemed like his

first link with reason since the sheriff had landed heavily on the deck of the *Sue Belle* that morning.

Lee looked from him to Miss Abbott—at her gentle face with faded blue eyes and soft white skin that reminded her of gardenia petals—then back at Johnny, who stared at his former teacher with hopeless eyes.

He stopped walking. "Do you know what they found on the *Sue Belle*, Miss Abbott?" His voice rose in disbelief.

She nodded and said as easily as if she were discussing logarithms, "I know all about the cocaine. We'll find out who put it there, Johnny."

Slowly his face split in a tremulous smile. "You don't think I put it there?"

"Don't be silly Johnny. You would never hide drugs on the *Sue Belle*. Never."

His smile faded and thick black eyebrows knotted in thought. "This bail stuff. I can't let you do that, Miss Abbott. I mean, I appreciate it and everything, but I guess I better wait 'til Dad gets home. I mean, he always said we had to take care of ourselves. When Mom died, he said it was the two of us together and we'd do for ourselves."

They were outside now standing on the sidewalk. He turned as if to go back inside.

"Wait, Johnny." He waited because it was a voice to be obeyed, a voice sure of command though in a gentle fashion.

"If your father were here," Miss Abbott said briskly, "he would post bond. He will handle everything when he gets home. But he wouldn't want you sitting in jail until he comes."

The boy looked at her with misery in his eyes. "What if Dad thinks I put that stuff there?" He stopped and his mouth quivered. "He trusted me with the *Sue Belle*. I'd never ever do anything to hurt the *Sue Belle*. I'd rather die. But what if he thinks it was me?" The enormity of the fear closed his throat.

"Johnny, don't be absurd. If I know and trust you," Miss Abbott smiled, "how much better does your father know and trust you?"

The boy nodded but his dark eyes stared somberly down the wide street. His dad knew him.

Lee imagined that Johnny was well aware his dad knew him lots better than Miss Abbott, knew some stupid, dumb things he'd done that he shouldn't have because everybody makes mistakes. Lee knew well that everybody does things that can haunt them. Maybe he'd lied sometime when he was out all night and wasn't with a friend like he said. There would be willing girls around boys like Johnny. Lee had brothers. She knew the trouble guys could get into. That was in Johnny's gaze.

Miss Abbot was brisk. "Johnny, did they feed you lunch?"

He slowly nodded.

"Did you eat?" she asked gently.

"No."

"That's our first stop. I haven't had lunch either and neither has Lee."

Johnny didn't look quite so stricken after he finished his second hamburger. Miss Abbott waited until he swallowed the last of his strawberry malt then she pulled a notebook and pen out of her purse.

They sat in the wooden booth in the small café and Miss Abbott set about her task of restoring order to Johnny's world. "It's time now that we considered our problem. Who put the cocaine on the *Sue Belle*? And why?"

For the first time, Johnny looked at the problem from the other end. He had seen it only as a calamity, an irrational happening that had engulfed him. Now his face creased in thought and he spoke almost as if to himself.

"Dad left Wednesday morning. I cleaned that locker out Thursday morning. There wasn't anything in it but an extra anchor chain on Thursday. So sometime between Thursday morning and this morning somebody put that block of cocaine in there."

He stopped as if listening to his own words, shook his head despondently. "It doesn't make sense. Why hide cocaine on the *Sue Belle*?"

Lee took another sip of iced tea. "Do you have a charter next week?"

"Dr. Cohen from Laredo. He's hired Dad for two weeks in June for seventeen years. Seventeen years," the boy repeated proudly.

"Oh," Lee said disappointedly, "Someone you know. I thought perhaps it could have been hidden aboard for pickup by your next charter."

Johnny didn't even have to think about that one. "Not Cohen. Huh-uh. That'd be crazy. He's rich. I mean, he's really rich. Why, he's got his own yacht bigger than our *Sue Belle* but he still charters us every summer. Says it reminds him of the first vacation he took, the year he finished his internship. Plus he knows Dad can always find tarpon. See, they like to follow a downfall and if you keep circling. . . ." His voice trailed off. Suddenly he was living in a world where there was no time to talk about how you troll for tarpon. No time. He frowned and said gruffly, "Not Dr. Cohen."

"When would you be likely to open that locker again?" Lee prodded.

Johnny shrugged. "Any time. No time. I might've put extra gear in there. I might not have opened it for weeks."

It was quiet for a moment and all of them tried to think

it out, tried to find some sort of pattern or logic in cocaine aboard the *Sue Belle*.

"Has anybody hired you for a trip up the coast anytime soon?" Miss Abbott asked.

That too was a dead end. No matter how they turned it up or down, the problem stayed like a paperweight with thick slow falling snowflakes misty and indistinct and unlikely.

They drank more iced tea and Johnny sucked on a Coke and tried to dredge up a reason, any sort of reason, and none came.

They walked out of the café into the bright afternoon, but they walked with shadows. On the drive back to Miss Abbott's shop, Lee asked abruptly, "Do you have any friends who might think the *Sue Belle* a good place to hide something, especially if they knew your father was out of town?"

"You mean like my friend Joe, the Cocaine Peddler?" Johnny almost grinned. "No way. I know kids who buy a joint or two but I don't know where the guys bought what they had." He rubbed the back of his neck and added a little stiffly. "I like beer."

Lee understood but she only smiled and said quietly, "So do I."

"All right then." Miss Abbott said briskly as she drove at a moderate pace down the narrow cement highway, "we don't see the block hidden for pickup or for safekeeping. But it was there and there has to be a reason."

They rode in silence the rest of the way to the ferry crossing. The ferry was midway across the channel when Miss Abbott said abruptly in an odd sort of voice, "We overlooked the most important point."

Johnny looked at her eagerly.

She sounded breathless. "Someone informed the police that the cocaine was aboard the *Sue Belle*."

Johnny's shoulders slumped. He said almost irritably, "We've known that all along."

"Oh," Lee said slowly, understanding dawning. "Of course. That changes everything."

Johnny was puzzled. "What's changed?"

"The point was not to sell the cocaine. The point was for the cocaine to be found on the *Sue Belle*. Someone deliberately tipped the sheriff's office."

"That is frightening," Lee said.

"Yes, "Miss Abbott agreed grimly.

Johnny shook his head again. "I don't get it. Why should anybody hide the stuff there then go call the police?"

His words hung in the air as the little ferry locked onto the ramp at Mustang Island.

Miss Abbott put the car in gear. As it pulled up onto the road, Johnny's face flattened.

"Yes, Johnny," she said quietly. "That's right. Somebody must not like you very much. Somebody wants you in jail."

Miss Abbott drove around to the back of the shops. As she parked Lee asked Johnny, "You said that you cleaned out that locker on Thursday. This is Saturday. So something prompted this in just the past few days."

Johnny, his face still shocked, looked at her numbly, "Everything's been regular. Except Dad being gone, of course."

"You are in someone's way, Johnny. That's what we have to figure out." Miss Abbott glanced at her watch. "I have an appointment with a customer at two." For an instant weariness pulled at her face. She took a deep breath. "I believe we've done all we can today." She looked at the blonde girl. "Lee, I can't thank you enough for coming and helping. You could easily have walked away."

Lee shook her head. Walk away from that shocked young

face? No. But she only said, "Nonsense. Now we have to find the person who—" She paused. "—has a grudge against Johnny."

"We shall," the older woman said determinedly. "Johnny, I want you to go home and sit down and write everything that has happened to you these past few days. Where you went, who you saw. Especially everything that happened aboard the *Sue Belle*."

"Yes, ma'am."

Lee new she could leave Johnny in safe hands, but she still wanted to help. The boy with the beautiful face was no longer an abstraction, a model for a drawing. He was a living feeling frightened person. "What time tomorrow?"

She was rewarded with a warm smile from Miss Abbott. "Let's say nine in the morning."

Lee was walking away from the parking lot when she heard Miss Abbott say sternly, "Remember, Johnny, everything that happened. Everything."

CHAPTER 7

Judy kept her eyes on the bread. They didn't have a slicer. She used a bread knife to cut thick pieces of the homemade white bread. A slice would be on the edge of every Blue Plate Special. Today's special was meat loaf, green beans, and mashed potatoes with cream gravy. Every time Mrs. Bailey stepped into the kitchen her voice was sharp and her face hard with a frown. Judy was painfully aware of the lump in the pocket of her skirt. She felt hot all over. Mrs. Bailey was mad because she was late. Over everything loomed the memory of the big man with the reddish hair and mustache. She remembered his tight grip on her arm when he demanded to know where she got the brooch. The brooch was a heavy weight in her pocket.

The café was open from eleven to seven every day but Sunday. Judy claimed a visiting aunt the week of Harry's vacation, otherwise she cleaned apartments early then worked in the café every day but Wednesday. Thursday, Friday, and Saturday were the busiest days, but she had Saturday mornings off since it always ran late to clean up after closing on Saturday. It was the delight of her week to take some of her tiny salary and go into Corpus Christi and shop. This had been a Saturday like all Saturdays. Except for the brooch. She wished she'd never seen the shiny bright piece. She finished slicing the bread.

Mrs. Bailey pointed at the refrigerator. "Hurry and clean more strawberries. We got a lot of orders for the strawberry shortcake. Then clear five and six."

Judy stood at the sink in the kitchen and cut stems off strawberries and washed them. Tears welled in her eyes. Mrs. Bailey didn't have to stay mad. She was only five minutes late. Well, maybe ten. But from the minute she hurried breathless into the café, Mrs. Bailey complained about people who didn't know how to keep a job and there was no way Judy would ever amount to anything if she wasn't dependable, interspersing the scolding with suspicious queries about the man in the sports car.

Judy said, "Man?"

"The man you were talking to in the fancy car. Who is he?"

Judy shook her head. "I don't know him. He asked me the way to the bus station."

"Is he from around here?"

Judy almost said no but she caught herself in time. "I don't know. I never saw him before today."

But the questions and the irritable outbursts about people who were late to work made Judy edgy. As she cleaned five and six, she froze for an instant every time the café door pushed in, afraid it might be the tall man who had gripped her arm so painfully hard in Corpus Christi. But he didn't come and finally the rush slowed. She stood in the hot kitchen and washed dishes. Stolen goods, that's what the big man said. She wiped a hot, wet hand across her face. She had to get rid of the brooch.

She stopped washing and her hands hung limply in the greasy water. What if Harry had already missed the brooch? She hadn't intended to take it and she would never even have touched it if she'd known it was anything special. There had been a heap of pretty yellow-colored pieces. Harry couldn't have known exactly how many pieces there were. Could he?

She scrubbed a skillet and remembered his heavy face and the way he looked up at the helicopter. She wouldn't want him to look at her like that. She'd better sneak the brooch back into Harry's apartment. It would be better to put it on the boat. That's where she'd found it. She hadn't intended to take it, but everything happened so quickly Friday. He didn't knock on the bottom of the boat. Instead, she heard him calling for her from over the side.

"Hey Judy, come here."

She was so startled she almost dropped her fishing rod. She jumped up and seen him bobbing in the water. What was wrong? A shark? She ran to the side of the boat. He pushed a basket up to the surface. "Grab hold of the handles, but be real careful." His light high voice sounded different than it ever had. More than just excited. He was triumphant.

Obediently, she reached out and grasped the wet wicker handles. She hauled the basket on board and wondered what was inside, but he was already pulling himself over the side and onto the deck. He grabbed the basket and carried it into the small cabin.

She saw him raise the lid to the tackle box, lift out a tray, and dump the contents of the basket into the box. He replaced the tray and shut the lid and was out on the deck and starting over the side when the sky was filled with the throbbing of a helicopter.

Harry stared up and his face was hard and ugly as the helicopter slipped down through the air to hover right above the motor boat. Judy covered her ears against the *whang* of the rotors. She wondered for a terrified instant if the helicopter was going to plunge down on the boat. The craft hung above them, heavy, loud, the wind from its rotors hot, then slowly lifted away.

When Judy looked out at the water, Harry was gone. That was when she made her mistake. Harry had disappeared down into the water. She had the boat to herself. Why was Harry so excited? She hurried to the tackle box and opened it and lifted out the tray. Her face curved in a smile at the heap of pretty things. She didn't stop to wonder how Harry could find jewelry on the ocean floor. She didn't think about value. She only thought the shining metal was pretty, so pretty.

She reached down and touched a golden turtle. It never occurred to her that it or any of the pretty things might be worth a fortune. She had seen rich people's jewelry in department stores. There was an entire section devoted to jewelry. Behind a glass case diamond rings glittered. Shiny bright silver and gold bracelets and necklaces gleamed in the light. Those things looked like money. The pieces tumbled in the tackle box were pretty but the metal had a soft almost dull look.

Judy stirred the little pile around. She picked up a golden bird and looked it over then laid it down to touch a funny shaped piece that looked like one of those Indian pictures. Her hand closed around it just as she heard the thump on the bottom of the boat.

Her heart thudded and she hurriedly replaced the inner tray and slammed down the lid and whirled to run to the center of the boat. She quickly scanned the horizon—no boats anywhere—then leaned down and knocked once to signal the all clear.

His reply knock sounded sharp and clear and she realized she still held the golden piece in her hand. She started back toward the cabin but there was no time. She heard Harry at the side of the boat. She jammed the piece in the pocket of her terrycloth beach robe and turned to face Harry.

There was never a chance to return the piece. After Harry unbuckled his tanks, he pulled on Levi's and a T-shirt, moving with desperate urgency. "We gotta get out of here. That 'copter could mean a Coast Guard boat will be out here quick, checking."

The boat bucketed over the water, leaving a churning wake. Judy held tight to a railing. When they pulled into the marina, Harry stopped at the dock just long enough to drop her off and then he had chugged back out into the channel, leaving her to get home the best way she could.

She felt then like she deserved the little piece and, when she got back to Mrs. Bailey's, she'd worked slowly and carefully taping a safety pin to the back of the little man, as she thought of him.

Now she washed the skillet and wondered how she was going to put the thing, that was how she called it in her mind, the thing, in Harry's apartment, find a place where he was keeping other stuff from the basket. Now that she knew the pieces were worth money to people, she was sure Harry wouldn't leave the jewelry in the boat. That wouldn't be safe. When she got off work from the café, she'd see if he was gone.

Mrs. Bailey put her to work mopping the kitchen floor when the dishes were finished, Judy mopped as fast as she could. She wanted to be free of the pin and all she could think to do was to put it in Harry's apartment. She would put the little man somewhere that Harry would think it had gotten snagged and carried along, like in that tacky old sweater he wore when the Gulf was cool. Or even toss it under his bed. Everything would be all right once she got rid of the brooch. She felt a little lurch deep inside. She yanked the piece from her pocket, feverishly removed the tape and the safety pin, then returned the piece to her pocket.

All afternoon she held fast to the idea of returning the jewel, as if that would somehow make it all right when she met the tall man tonight. Maybe he would leave her alone when he knew she had put it back. She didn't want to meet him, but she knew she had to or he would come storming up to Nightingale Courts demanding to talk to her. Judy knew that if Mrs. Bailey ever found out she'd taken a jewel, Mrs. Bailey would fire her.

It was almost five o'clock when she walked tiredly out of the kitchen and down the back steps of the café. There was silence in Nightingale Courts. The sun was hot and the harsh glow made the pink stucco looked ever more faded.

Judy walked slowly along the paved walk in front of the converted motel rooms. His beat-up old Plymouth wasn't in the slot. Her heart thudded but she was eager. She walked a little faster. Pretty soon everything was going to be all right. Her hand slid to her pocket for the ring with keys to the apartments. She looked furtively around. No one stirred in the late afternoon heat. Mrs. Bailey was probably in her place, drinking tea and resting.

Judy stopped in front of Harry's door. If anyone saw her going in and told Mrs. Bailey, she'd have to explain and what could she say? The apartments were done once a week in the mornings. There was no reason for her to go into Harry Cassell's apartment now.

She'd seen Harry at the café early and he'd not said a word to her. She thought likely he was off in the big trailer, maybe on a run to Mexico. He often went to Mexico.

Judy pulled the ring of keys from her pocket, stepped close to the door, unlocked it, pushed hurriedly inside. Once inside, she closed the door behind her and turned on the living room light. She waited for the trembling of her legs to stop. Now that she was inside, she realized that she would have to come out again. That would be worse. How could she know whether the parking lot was empty? What if she opened the door and stepped out to meet Mrs. Bailey?

Tears burned and she rubbed her eyes harshly. She was so

hot and tired. Too much had happened and tonight she must face that big determined man. She took one deep breath and then another and pulled the pin out of her pocket. She hurried across the room to the bedroom and stepped in. She turned on the light. The bed wasn't made. Clothes straggled over the one chair. She darted to the closet and twisted the knob. The closet door was locked.

Why would he lock his closet door? Blocked there, she looked frantically around the room and the throbbing in her head worsened. There was no place to put the golden piece.

Once a week she ran the sweeper in this room but for the first time she truly saw it. He had lived in it for five years. A comb and a hairbrush rested on top of the dresser. Nothing else. A lamp sat on the table next to the easy chair. The only color in the room came from the row of magazines stacked along the north wall.

A green metal footlocker near the window caught her eye. She crossed to it and knelt then stared hopelessly at the shiny padlock that hung in the hasp.

Suddenly, brutal fingers clamped onto her shoulder, pulling her up and away from the footlocker, shoving her backwards.

She fell heavily against the wall. Her left shoulder and elbow took the full force of the impact. The pin spun free from her hand. Even in her pain and fear she knew she mustn't lose the pin. He must not see the golden piece. She tried to scramble forward. She flung herself across the floor and her right hand scrabbled for the irregularly shaped oblong of gold.

Her fingers were curling over it when he finished checking the padlock on the footlocker and turned to watch her. He moved quickly for a stocky man. His boot pressed her wrist to the floor. The pressure pulled her fingers back.

The jewel lay in clear view.

She lay there, her face against the slick yellow wood, her arm outstretched, trembling with pain and fear. Then the pressure on her wrist abruptly eased. He yanked her to her feet. He held her arms in a vicious grip.

"I was bringing it back," she gasped, her voice high and ragged. 'I was bringing it back. I didn't know it was anything important 'til the man came after me. I promised him I'd put it back."

His broad face wavered in front of her teary eyes, but she saw the hard ridge of muscle in his jaw and the line of sweat beading his mouth. "Man?" His high voice was sharp and breathless. "Man? God damn you, what man?"

He held her so hard she wanted to scream but her throat was dry and swollen. He shook her until her head lolled back and forth like a rag doll.

"What man?"

His voice was as light and deadly as the crackle of leaves when a rattlesnake slithers by.

CHAPTER 8

Harry stood, his back against the door, and stared at the lengthening rectangular stripe of sunlight probing deeper and deeper into the room. The longer the strip of sunlight, the later it was in the day. It would be getting close to six o'clock now but the blood-red sun wouldn't be gone from view for at least another two and a half hours. It wouldn't be dark until eight-thirty. He watched the bar of sunlight. His eyes clung to the stripe of light but his thoughts split and met and parted like marbles flung on a linoleum floor. He couldn't seem to stop the rolling and tumbling.

A hundred pictures wavered in his mind, one merging into another, some dim, some bold and clear. Across the years he could see the tiny crowded room and the flickering light of a gas stove and diapers strung over it to dry. Winter rain hissed against the windows. The rain swept inside when the door opened. His father stumbled in. Harry was nine years old and he already knew enough to pull back into the shadow of the room and make himself small. He knew the smell and the thick loud voice and the way his mother screamed when the blows began. He swore that when he grew up, he'd never get "laid off," that no matter what happened, he wouldn't be shamed.

When he was ten, he got a job sweeping out at Mr. Hodak's barber shop. That was where he saw the gleam of gold coins piled high on the cover of a magazine. Mr. Hodak booted him in the rear and told him he wasn't paid to read. He'd been careful after that, sneaking out the magazines, reading slowly, laboriously, his finger pushing the words along. The enchanted world of treasure became as real to him as the smell of coal smoke and the whistle of the freights. He moved through his days, stocky and strong, polite enough if you spoke to him, but his light blue incurious eyes touched the speaker for a moment, then move back to their secret thoughts.

He was drafted after he finished high school. He moved through his days in Vietnam heavily and quietly. He shot gooks when he was told to and crinkled his face in puzzlement the night a private cried because he'd killed a man that day. After that, Harry made sure he never moved out on patrol beside that kid. His only thought had been that when you killed somebody, they sure couldn't hurt you any.

When he got out of the Army, he used the job training to go to one of the big truck driving schools. He took the job with Pan-Con because Corpus was close to Padre Island.

All these years he'd read about Padre Island, but he'd never seen it. The first day he saw the Island was the worst day of his life. He'd read everything he could find about millions of dollars' worth of gold shipwrecked off Padre and buried on Padre. Reading had never come easy to him but he'd read all the books and studied the maps. It looked so clear and easy on the maps, Four Mile Hill and Big Hill and Little Dagger Hill, Green Hill, Dagger Hill, Big Ball Hill, Lone Hill, Little Shell Beach, Devil's Elbow, Black Hill, Big Shell Beach, and on and on. Little arrows marked sites where ships went down.

He held a map that day. He'd taken the ferry to Port Aransas and followed the shore dive until he was on Padre and then he continued to drive on the hard-packed sand of the beach. He drove for twenty miles, maybe twenty-five miles, before he stopped the car. He stared at unending sand dunes with prickly matted coverings of dune grass and sunflowers.

He'd been a fool. This hill or that hill, hell! He looked again at the map and the snake-like line of the Island. Padre Island was a hundred and ten miles long and varied in width from two to five miles. He looked up from the map. Two to five miles across. Wide firm beaches and huge dunes fifteen, twenty, forty feet high. Maybe there was treasure under some of the dunes but he could carry a metal detector up and down one dune and spend his life doing it and when he was through he'd have a pile of bottle caps and beer cans and spent shells.

He got out of the car and stared at endless rugged dunes with patches of white shifting sand and coarse grasses and cactus and desert flowers.

A dream died.

Harry read all the books and he believed every one (*Ten Steps to Riches, Where The Treasure Is, You, Too, Can Be Rich*). Buried treasure, the dream of the ages. He crumpled the map in his hand. Then he turned and looked out at the flat calm blue water. Not all the treasure was hidden on the Island. There was treasure out in the water.

He was a good truck driver, nerveless, steady. He made good money. He soon learned on his trips down into Mexico that a man with steady nerves could earn even more money by bringing in a little extra cargo for a friend. He worked and he smuggled and he earned money for a boat, the *Lucky Lady*. He learned to scuba dive. He learned about fathometers and shoals and flats and buoys.

Now he stood in his shabby room, the treasure found and

watched the bar of sunlight move closer. A deep corroding bitterness twisted his face.

Damn them. Damn them all. Everybody always all the time trying to louse him up. He hunted for five years. Every free day. Summer. Winter. Hot. Cold. Men o'war stung him. He faced down a stalking shark. He was so close when those people from Indiana with their money and equipment found one of the galleons and brought the things up, load after load. He laughed when the state seized the artifacts but the laughter shrilled to fury when the new law came out. Now every artifact recovered off Padre Island belonged to the State of Texas. Only somebody with a license could dive for treasure and licenses would go only to archeologists and approved salvage groups.

It wasn't fair. Florida hadn't made a lousy law like that and those people off the Florida coast had made at least two million dollars from the galleons they found.

Harry didn't stop diving. The law just made searching harder, always having to keep an eye out for state agents.

He found his galleon in April. That was how he thought of the wreckage. His galleon. He learned a lot in the years he searched. He read more books, better books. He learned how ships foundering and splitting apart in a storm are likely to break up and how a trail of ballast balls can lead to other barnacle-encrusted humps of debris. He learned how four hundred years of submersion in sea water electrolyzes wood and iron and silver. The sea remakes everything but gold. Only gold remained unsullied. Other artifacts could be saved with immersions in carefully calculated baths but gold, pure gold, retains its nature. He learned that the value of ancient navigational aides is fantastic.

And he learned to be artful in his comings and goings. After he found his galleon, he was careful not to vary his routine, careful not to make special purchases close to home, careful not to stir the interest of the many adventurers who hungrily nosed up and down the Island, alert for the merest hint of discovery.

He could lose his treasure in two ways: to the government or to anybody bigger and tougher who could take it away from him.

Right from the first, things had broken wrong. That skinny guy who tried to act like it was his find. Harry hadn't had any choice. If that punk had ever reached land and told anybody, Harry could kiss his treasure goodbye. Then there was that nosy old man at the marina. Harry felt sure he had turned the *Lucky Lady* into the state as a possible treasure hunter. Why else had that helicopter swept down on Friday to hover right above the boat? And it was on Friday that Harry really found the goods. He needed to make at least one more dive. At least one more.

The lengthening bar of sunlight reached the thick gleaming blackness of Judy's hair. He stared at the tumbled heap of hair and saw with dull surprise how her hair still glistened in the sunlight.

It was her own fault. Taking the piece. Wearing it. Letting a big stranger see it, a man who knew what it was, who was determined to find where it came from. He pulled his eyes away from the gleaming black locks. She led the man straight to Nightingale Courts. Stupid. When she didn't show up at the end of the boardwalk tonight, the man would come here. Once he came, Harry was doomed.

He took a half breath, trying to pull air past the fear that thickened his throat. They'd put him in jail. They'd take his treasure.

Harry rubbed his face and felt a faint repulsion at sticky patches where sweat had cooled to chilly clamminess. That's when he realized that he was cold. His damp shirt clung to him; he shuddered. Furiously he clenched his powerful hands. He had to move. He had to think.

Judy. The man.

He looked at the clock, Six. Dinnertime. Mrs. Bailey knew he was here. He always ate at the café when he was in town. If he didn't go for dinner, she would wonder why.

He wiped his hands on the front of his jeans. He couldn't walk out of here and Judy crumpled on the floor like that.

The minute hand jerked. Five after six.

He reached his hand behind him to make sure that latch was turned. He moved to the closet, pulled out a key, opened the door. A stack of Army blankets was on a low shelf. He bought the blankets at an army surplus store in Austin when he began his forays out of Aransas Pass to buy the hundred and one things he needed to haul up and clean and hide his treasure. He knew many of his purchases would mark him suspect among the hungry drifters who waited for news of an illegal treasure strike, waited and watched with the greed and ferocity of vultures.

He grabbed a blanket. He was thinking straight now. Wool doesn't hold fingerprints. Turning back into the room, he opened the blanket out on the floor, awkwardly rolled the inert body onto it. He folded the blanket over her and pulled the lumpy bundle into the closet. He locked the closet.

Outside, heat struck him like a furnace blast. He sweated as he walked the short distance from the apartment to the café. He settled at the counter as he often did.

Mrs. Bailey slammed back the swinging door from the kitchen. Her white curls hung in limp disorder. Rivulets of perspiration eroded her makeup base. Her navy-blue dress clung damply. "Young people aren't to be trusted. I should have known that." She thumped down a huge platter of fried chicken on a serving station, glanced at Harry. "Special tonight is fried chicken, mashed potatoes, gravy, peas."

"Special sounds good." Harry thought he sounded fine, just like usual. "Iced tea."

She served him a plate, wiped her face. "I forgot the rolls," and turned to go into the kitchen.

Harry took his napkin and neatly spread it in his lap.

Mrs. Bailey carried the bowl of rolls in her left hand. In her right, she gripped the handle of the heavy tea pitcher. She poured Harry a glass, put the pitcher down. "I thought Judy was happy here. I really did." Tears brimmed in her faded puzzled brown eyes.

Harry looked around the cafe. "Isn't Judy here?"

Mrs. Bailey shook her head. She tried to speak but her lips trembled. She rubbed her face with her hands. "I got too hot. Judy's worked most lunch and dinners since she came. I haven't had to work so hard. We always had such a cheerful time, cleaning up. Now she's gone. She didn't say a word about being unhappy, not a word."

She looked around the café, almost every seat taken, usually a sight to please her. "It's a man, of course. It's always a man." Her mouth pinched in at the corners. "I didn't think that man in the sports car was a stranger like she said. He talked too much to be asking the way."

"Man?" Harry asked, his voice high and soft and light.

Mrs. Bailey nodded heavily. "Just before noon. I saw the car; one of those little blue foreign cars. It turned in as she came down the drive and pulled up beside her. She looked so guilty when she saw me watching. She turned back to him and pointed up the street like she was giving directions but I thought then that it looked funny. Now she's gone. She isn't here anywhere. There's no note but she's never missed helping with dinner on Saturday night. She knows it's my big night."

"I saw a blue car up the street about five o'clock," Harry said softly.

Mrs. Bailey's face hardened, but there was a little twitching quiver in her right cheek. "Well, it's all you can expect. A girl like that." The older woman hurried to serve up several specials, said over her should to him as she walked out with the plates, "I thought she liked it here."

Back in his apartment, Harry waited patiently for night. Everything would be all right as long as he kept his head. At eight-thirty he decided it was dark enough. He changed to dark clothes. He unlocked the closet stepped over the hump of the blanket, and picked up the .22 rifle standing in the corner.

He held the gun by his thumb and forefinger until he could lay it on his bed. He went to the top drawer of the dresser and lifted out a pair of canvas gloves, a box of .22 shells and a chamois. He put on the gloves and polished the rifle with the chamois. He polished slowly and carefully and he didn't miss any of the blue-black metal or the cheap plastic stock. It wasn't much of a gun. He'd won it in a poker game in Monterrey while he was on a layover, waiting for his truck to be loaded for the return trip. He'd taken it out on the Island a couple of times and pinged beer cans and gulls. A .22 caliber bullet can kill a rabbit or a squirrel or a horse or a man if it strikes a vulnerable spot.

His target wouldn't be moving.

He polished the rifle and loaded it. It was only a single-action rifle, but he wouldn't need more than one shot. He stuck the box of shells in his right pants pocket, opened the door a fraction, and turned off the light. He stood in his darkened room, waiting for the pupils of his eyes to expand and listening to the night sounds around Nightingale Courts. A far away siren. Some laughter from a passing car. Harry stepped out, shutting the door behind him. He started up the sidewalk.

A door three units up opened. One of the old ladies who lived there started out. He eased backward into the shadow of a trellis.

A wavering voice called out, “Don’t be silly, Sister. It can wait until morning. Come back in here.”

Harry waited until the door closed. Gripping the rifle, he walked fast to his car, eased the door open, slid into the driver’s seat. He propped the rifle on the passenger seat. No one could say they’d seen him with a rifle. There would be a full moon but it would not rise until long past midnight. Now, it was dark.

He slipped out of the car, walked around to the trunk. He unlocked it. Lifted the lid. The interior light flashed on. Damn, he’d forgotten about the light. He reached in, traced the wire, yanked it out. He slowly lowered the lid, left it resting unlocked.

It was a cool evening, but he was beginning to sweat. It was taking too long. Everything was taking too long. He walked fast down the sidewalk, fast but quiet, to his apartment door, unlocked it. Inside, the door shut, he checked the time. Eighteen minutes to nine.

The man would be at the end of the boardwalk at nine o’clock.

Harry unlocked the closet. He reached down and tried to lift the long rolled hump of blanket. Panic suffused him as hot and weakening as fever. Judy’s body had begun to stiffen. When he managed to pick up the hideously heavy shape, it stretched firm and straight and would not sag and bend. He stood, trapped in the closet, the shoulders and knees of the body unyielding against the frame of the narrow doorway.

For a moment terror crowded against him. He pulled for air with deep gasping breaths, all the while pushing the stiff heavy blanket-swathed body against the immovable wood. Sweat streaming down his face, he swung the body upright and stumbled through the door.

He was running out of time. What if the man left the boardwalk before he got there? The man would stay. He thought he was going to lay his hands on a fortune. He wouldn't leave the boardwalk.

Harry smiled a little at that. The man wouldn't leave the boardwalk. Not ever.

Harry opened the front door, looked out. He wouldn't hurry now. If he hurried now, if he made a mistake now, he was finished. He listened. The parking area was quiet. The TV next door blared. Cars passed on the street. He stepped out, propped the body against the wall, as he locked the door, lifted it again, long and stiff. Judy was heavy. Heavier now than she'd ever been in life.

He was halfway to his car when he heard footsteps. Dragging, agonizingly slow steps. Mrs. Bailey, shoulders slumped, shuffled on the far side of the lot, walking from the back of the café toward her unit that backed on the alley.

He stood absolutely still, his grisly bundle propped against the wall.

Mrs. Bailey came to a stop.

A passing car turned into the lot. The headlights swept over him, blinding him for a moment.

Mrs. Bailey whirled around. "Judy?" the old voice quavered hopefully. "Judy, is that you?"

The car's tires squealed as it backed and turned to go into the street in the other direction.

Harry slowly laid his grotesque bundle on the ground.

"Judy? Judy?"

"Mrs. Bailey?" he called. He moved slowly out of the shadow of the honeysuckle. He could see Mrs. Bailey's shoulders sag.

"Mr. Cassell? A car turned in. I thought maybe. . . ." Her words trailed off.

"Just somebody turning around."

"Have you been out here long?"

"No, ma'am. I'm loading my car. I'm going night fishing."

"You haven't. . . . I mean, you didn't see anyone else out here?" She hesitated then asked in a rush, "You haven't seen Judy, have you?"

"No, ma'am."

He waited until she reached her unit, opened the door, closed it behind her. He hurried back to the shadows, hefted the heavy burden. It didn't take long to lift the trunk lid, dump the body, and slam the lid shut.

He drove carefully the seven miles to the ferry crossing. On Saturday night the ferries ply steadily back and forth across the hundred-yard width of the channel carrying campers, swimmers, fishermen, picnickers.

Harry was in a long line. Finally, the car thumped onto the ferry. On the other side, he saw the long straggling line of cars ahead of him and his hands gripped the steering wheel impatiently. He looked down at his watch: three minutes to nine. He couldn't get there for another fifteen minutes. Maybe twenty. What if the man jumped in his sports car and hurtled across the island and onto the ferry and raced right up to Nightingale Courts and yelled for Judy?

The thick flow of cars picked up a little speed but he knew there would be traffic all along the main way. He planned to dump Judy close to where Judy said the man was staying, La Casa Hermosa, but the time was closing in. It didn't matter anyway as long as she was found on Mustang Island and Bailey told police she'd run off in a blue sports car. Harry would be safe then. The man wouldn't be around to explain. The dead girl linked to a dead man wouldn't make sense to the cops, but the crazier the facts, the less likely anything would lead to Harry.

The White Marlin Restaurant loomed ahead. Harry twisted the wheel and took a cut-off road, a rarely traveled blacktop that curved across scrubby flatland and linked up with the main street on the other side of the island.

Midway across the island he checked the rearview mirror, then braked hard. He was out of the car and at the trunk in seconds. Quickly, quickly, he unlocked the trunk and reached inside.

Dead weight. Heavy, heavy, heavy. He yanked and pulled. Any minute, any second, a car could turn into the cutoff. With a desperate heave, he hauled the stiffening body out, stumbled a few feet away from the road and threw the bundle into a scrub-grass shrouded depression.

Someone out early, a birdwatcher, a milkman, a jogger, would find the contorted body but it wouldn't matter.

He slammed down the trunk, ran to the front, jumped in. He threw the engine in gear and was on his way.

One more stop to make and he'd be safe.

CHAPTER 9

Dan looked at his watch. Thirteen minutes after nine.

He turned on his heel, paced eight steps forward, eight back. The worn weathered gray-brown wood of the boardwalk creaked under his weight. He paused under a spill of light from the lamppost near the end of the boardwalk and peered blindly out into the night. He couldn't see past the boundary of the light. Irritably, he swung again into his tense back-and-forth pacing.

His face was twisted in an unaccustomed scowl. Why had he let the girl go? Sap Holloway, that's who he was! Coming all over softhearted when she turned those great frightened black eyes on him. Why the hell hadn't he grabbed the ornament when he had the chance?

"You dumb son of a bitch," he growled at himself. Within arm's reach of a priceless magnificent artifact of pre-Columbian Mexico and he was empty-handed. He knew the piece was a temple relic, perhaps worn by the high priest on special days of offering.

His pace slowed. During the interminable afternoon, he sketched—in as exact a fashion as possible—the ornament he glimpsed that morning on the softly rounded breast.

He stopped at the periphery of the lamppost's glow and visualized the pin again, the soft indescribable sheen of old gold, the incredible detail of a tiny golden pot of incense with the sinuous length of a snake protruding from the spout.

His eyebrows pulled down in thought. Did the conical cap have extrusions to make it look like ocelot skin? That would fit in with the likely iconography. Had he truly seen upraised swirls on the golem representing the markings of the husky cat? Or had he mistaken the glitter of the gold for repousse?

He shrugged. That point didn't particularly matter. He had a good picture of the golden god in his mind and in his notebook and they told him a fantastic tale. He was certain no one had dug this up from a pirate's cache or found it while strolling down the beach. The ornament was not Spanish gold. It was not colonial craftsmanship. It was somehow, in some miraculous fashion, a survivor of the ages before Cortes and his men broke the back of the Aztec Empire. Dan had seen, if only for an instant what must have been a relic from temple days before Cortes.

Therefore, the golden piece should never have been on Padre Island. That it *was* here meant one thing only—that the bones of another galleon had been found and the ship must have carried, in addition to the usual mined and minted tonnage of gold and silver, a collection of Aztec temple goods.

It must, in fact, be the archeological discovery of the decade. Perhaps the discovery of the century because so few relics had survived from pre-Columbian days.

His mind toyed delicately, in a playful fashion, with the fabled stories of Montezuma's treasure, the treasure of the House of Azayacatl, lost and gone for four hundred and fifty years. His scholar's skepticism totted up the years between the Noche Triste and the treasure fleet of 1553 that went aground off Padre. Thirty-three years. Too long. But it was a beautiful thought. When he saw the artifact again, he would know. He looked at his watch. Seventeen minutes after nine.

A sense of urgency, of failure tightened his nerves. He began to pace again, head thrust forward, shoulders leaning as if he moved against a hard wind.

He felt a hard whuff of hot air. It raised a thick tuft of his auburn hair at the back of his head. The instantly identifiable crackle of a shot was followed by a ping as the shell struck the metal rim of the protective shade around the bulb at the top of the lamppost.

Dan knew the sound of shots. Bigger ones but none ever that close. He lunged forward, his legs thrusting hard against the boardwalk, and hurtled over the railing. It would have made a beautiful last-minute block. The only problem was that no obliging halfback was waiting to take the impact, leaving Dan to absorb the force of his fall all by himself. His long limbs were sheathed by tidy spare muscles. No loose fat. No sagging pouches. No softening layers.

A dozen thoughts pummeled his mind as his body made its instinctual plunge for safety. The girl? Surely the girl wasn't shooting at him. But the shot had to be tied to the ornament. This proved he had stumbled into something big. He was dead if he didn't get out of the light. Dead. The bullet *pinged* on the lamppost shade. That meant an upward trajectory. Shooting up? The gunman was in the gully. Dan was falling into the gully.

He landed hard. His right shoulder took the greater force of the impact. A shock of pain immobilized him for an instant. Despite the hot lick of a torn ligament, he scrabbled backwards, pushing with his palms against tough dune grass, driving his body backward. He braced for a bullet the whole time as he scrambled to get out of the circle of light.

Cactus spines tore along his body. His right leg burned with a hundred tiny punctures but he reached blessed darkness. He pulled up into a crouch, lunged to his left. He ran a half dozen steps then tripped over a tangle of vines. He catapulted head first into a stand of sunflowers whose giant stalks stretched up to a height of eight or nine feet. The stalks crumpled beneath him. He lay in the midst of the thicket trying to breathe without rasping, trying to hear above the rustle of the sunflowers and the unceasing roar of the sea.

Why didn't the gunman shoot again as he plunged off the boardwalk. The first shot *pinged* against the lamppost shade. Dan should have been a clear target as he tumbled off the boardwalk into the gully between the dunes. If the gunman didn't want to risk a mid-air shot, why not a bullet as Dan scrambled desperately, awkwardly, like a terrified crab to reach the darkness?

Dan lay tensely among the sunflower stalks. He smelled the musky, faintly aromatic scent of the huge plants, felt their sandpapery texture against his bare arms. He tried to work it out. He was pretty sure the rifle was a . Nothing else sounded quite like a .22. As for the lack of a second shot, could that mean a single-action rifle? Would a killer come out to hunt a man with a single-action rifle?

A woman might. A damn-fool woman just might. Or a man with an arrogant certainty of his aim. Or somebody desperate to kill and a single-action .22 was the only weapon at hand.

Eyes narrowed, Dan searched the shadow-pocked valley that ran between two big dunes. The shot came from the other side of the boardwalk but the gunman could be anywhere by now. Dan looked up the sides of the dunes but saw nothing but shadows.

A dozen marksmen could be in place along the ridge of the dune, all prone, all ready. He was a fish in a barrel down here in the gully.

The sniper would be waiting for movement, for the giveaway rattle of leaves, the shush of shifting sand.

Dan moved the fingers of his right hand, the tip ends seeking like antennas. He felt the abrasive but furry sunflower leaves, sharp-edged blades of grass, hard lumpy mounds of shells. He didn't dare move his body forward or back. The tall sunflowers would rustle and pinpoint him as exactly as the green blip on a radar reveals an airplane.

His questing fingers passed over broken edges of hundreds of sea shells and then his hand curved over an egg hell. He fit his hand around the curve of the shell, probably from an abalone, and waited. He listened harder than he'd ever listened before, harder than the night he'd crouched wet and surrounded in a rice paddy, harder than the night he'd led a patrol out into sapper territory Those nights had been bad but the danger had been an all-pervading, mind-chilling general danger. This was a specific personal danger. Somewhere nearby, probably on the ridge of a dune, someone waited with the sole object of shooting Dan Holloway.

He waited and listened and then slowly he rolled his weight onto his left side, freeing his right arm and shoulder. He threw the shell at the boardwalk. The abalone shell hit a shadowy portion of the boardwalk then fell with a clatter into a mound of broken-up shells. The sharp shallow crack of the .22 sounded from almost directly above Dan, right along the highest point of the dune.

Dan was up on his feet and running in a mad scrambling lunge up the side of the dune, tangling in the long flat tendrils of dune grass, slipping when sand shifted under the force of his weight, gambling that the shooter held a single-action rifle, knowing that he might be wrong.

He bulled his way up the uncertain slope. He'd never liked a defensive posture and he damn sure wasn't going to go down without a fight.

He felt a hot angry flush of pleasure as he neared the top. His gamble paid off. He had a chance for no shot had come. The killer had a single-action and was trying to reload as Dan charged.

Dan was just short of the ridge when he saw a dark figure against the horizon. He sensed the brutal swing almost before it began.

Dan had run out of choices when he began his desperate ascent, so he clawed his way to the top and jumped forward, head down, shoulders tensed. He butted his adversary and relished the agonized explosive exhalation of his enemy.

The rifle didn't hit Dan with full force but the barrel struck hard enough to break his grip on his attacker. They both fell. Dan landed halfway down the slope, tumbling out of control, rolling sideways down the dune, grasping unsuccessfully at tufts of grass. His adversary crashed heavily somewhere ahead of him.

Dan jolted to a stop at the bottom of the dune. He pushed himself up, listening for movement, for sound, for the click of a bolt. He pushed up and tried to run but the soft sand shifted beneath his feet. His quarry was ahead of him, running away. They were far from the lighted boardwalk. Not even the gleam of starlight penetrated the clouds to give any light. Lightning flared briefly, palely, like a fleeting reflection on a mirror in a darkened room. For an instant beneath the darkness of rain-laden clouds, the dunes rose up and down, pale images of the golden sands of the day. Thunder rumbled in the southwest. In the purplish glow from a larger flash of lightning, Dan saw a stocky hunched figure struggling up a dune about twenty-five yards ahead.

Dan forgot the thrumming ache in his side, the pricks and scratches from the cactus, the warning twinge in his ankle that augured trouble to come. He poured on the speed. Even in the darkness of night on bad terrain, a good runner has reserves. His knees pulled high but naturally so. He ran solidly, hard and fast, remembering the obstacles briefly revealed in the lightning flash.

He was gaining on his quarry. He heard the strained rasp of winded breathing. Dan ran a little harder and then his toe caught on a piece of driftwood and he was thrown forward. He had just topped a dune so there was no place to go but down, a long way down. If it hadn't been sand he would have been maimed for life. He literally flew through the air. He fought to get his legs down, to take the impact on his knees and forearms but it was his shoulder again and this time he couldn't get up for a long moment. He struggled to pull air down into his lungs and endured the rending flash of pain that shocked through him.

When he could raise his head, he realized with a dreadful coldness that he no longer heard the man ahead of him. Ahead of him? He could be anywhere. And there had been time and enough to reload that single-action rifle.

Dan moved his head very slowly, very carefully. He was right back where he'd started from. Just a little tireder, a little slower. Once again, he had his tail in a crack lying at the bottom of a dune. He needed elevation, a chance to see. Slowly, carefully, he began to crawl upward.

CHAPTER 10

For a long moment after the lightning flash, Lee could see nothing. The darkness seemed doubly black in contrast to that brilliant streak of silvery light. Gradually the pupils of her eyes widened as she adjusted to the darkness. She sat in the miniature widow's walk atop the beach house and relaxed, her mind drifting obliquely from one thought to another.

Every evening since her arrival she climbed the wooden stairs to the plank-seated observation post. The walk was patterned after the rooftop walks that New England sea captains' wives paced, looking out toward the steely surging Atlantic and hoping.

Suddenly a multipronged bolt of lightning, fangs of fire flickering in white brilliance, blazed in the southern sky. Thunder exploded. Even though she knew the storm was coming, the tremendous volley of sound impressed her. In the quiet that followed, she heard a sharp pop. Almost immediately, the flat shallow sound was followed by another wham of thunder. Suddenly she saw sheets of rain sweeping toward shore across roiling water. That brief glimpse of the surging sea awed her and she wondered at the bravery and skill of those who weather storms at sea.

She was halfway down the wooden steps to the balcony when the rain struck the cabin and she remembered that she hadn't rolled up the windows of the VW. Normally, it wouldn't matter too much because even a heavy rain wouldn't hurt the sturdy vinyl seat covers but she had borrowed some books from the paperback lending library and she'd left them on the front seat when she hauled in groceries.

She gained the shelter of the living room and hesitated. If she didn't retrieve them, the books would be a mess. Many responsibilities she could shirk: a promise to drop in at a cocktail party, a pledge to get together soon at the Faculty Club, attendance at a visiting guest lecture to bolster the department turnout. About those sorts of things, she could fuzz and fudge and show a distinct lack of character. But to leave books to molder in the rain, their pages turning into sodden lumps, their covers wilting? She couldn't do it.

She hurried across the dark living room and out the door. The steps led down to the sand beneath the beach house. Even under the beach house the rain gusted. Lee was shocked at the wind's chill and the pellet-like force of the rain. She wished she had taken time to pull on her raincoat but she knew she must get the books now or they would be past saving. She dashed out into the swirling rain.

She was only a few feet from the VW when an arm closed roughly around her throat and a hand grabbed her right arm and pulled it behind her back. A hard voice began, "That's it, fella, you're all done."

Lee's heart pumped erratically. Her left hand scratched at the arm around her neck. As abruptly as she had been caught, she was freed. She gasped for breath. "What are you doing here?"

"Be quiet." The voice was no longer harsh but it was peremptory, commanding.

Oddly enough she did as she was told.

The man moved a little nearer, whispered, "Get down. There's a guy out there with a gun."

His hand pulled impatiently at her arm. She hesitated. Then the hand tightened and yanked, pulled her down. An arm clamped over her shoulders. Before she could struggle, a voice murmured irritably in her ear, "Stop wiggling and listen. A man with a gun is close. He's trying to kill me. He's shot at me three times. I was trying to jump him and I mistook you for him. Don't get up and run or scream. He's had time to reload and he might get you instead of me." With no further word, he eased his grip but lay close beside her with a light hand on her shoulder.

Lee remembered Queen Victoria who never deigned to look behind her when she shot out her dainty feet to sit in a chair. The chair would be there, of course. It always had been. It always would be. Did he automatically assume that when he spoke, he would be obeyed?

Torn between tears of anger and relief, Lee felt a tiny smile quirk her mouth. The arrogant male. Sure of his command. She had been instructed to be quiet. She would, of course, be quiet.

She tensed when he moved closer, so close she could feel the length of his leg pressed against her and the heavy pressure of his shoulder. His mouth touched her ear and she felt the scratch of a mustache.

"I apologize," he whispered, his breath warm and soft against her face. "I'm sorry I jumped you. You see, I was tracking this fellow and I lost him. I saw movement near the beach house. It was you, of course, but I didn't know that. Since the place was dark, I thought no one was home."

"That's quite all right," she whispered in return. As she listened to her words, however, and felt the warmth of his body next to hers and the penetrating cold of the rain, she thought wildly that this moment must all be a hallucination. She could not possibly be stretched out on sharp-edged shells and wet sand calmly talking to one man about how another was trying to kill him.

He was quiet now, his apology made.

Lee, so accustomed to fending her way, so used to making her own judgments, sensed concentration, felt the slight withdrawal of his warmth next to her.

When he said a moment later, "I'd better see you safely indoors," a touch of impatience in his voice, she knew immediately that he considered her a burden and a responsibility to be disposed of.

Her response was a conditioned one, she knew, but she made it nevertheless. "That's perfectly all right," she whispered crisply. "You needn't trouble yourself." She might be dismissing a colleague's offer to see her safely home from a faculty cocktail party. She began to get up on her hands and knees.

Abruptly she was shoved flat. He whispered angrily, "Don't be a damned fool."

She managed to turn her head under the iron-hard pressure of his arm to hiss, "Does your little man with a gun have infrared vision? It is utterly black. It is raining heavily, to use a weatherman's favorite term. I cannot, for example, see you. Yet, believe me, I know you are there."

The arm that pressed her down into the broken shells and sand was abruptly moved.

"Lady, when they start drafting women then women will learn a little respect for guns. Now if you don't mind the polite suggestion of an old infantryman, how about you keep your bottom down and crawl toward your house."

If she could have seen his face, she would have slapped it with a good deal of pleasure. But if somebody with a gun was out there, and she believed somebody was, then perhaps she should keep her bottom down.

She had never crawled anywhere before. Presumably she had progressed in infancy from leg waving to some sort of crawl but that was mercifully far in her past. As she inched toward the beach house on her hands and knees, bottom down, she marveled at the stamina of the average baby. Babies were not, of course, expected to crawl in the pitch dark over uneven sand matted with wiry, sharp-bladed grasses and mounds of broken shells. Her scratched knees stung. Her back ached. She was freezing. But she crawled doggedly on. She'd be damned if she'd even pause with Captain Heroic coming along behind.

They reached the shelter beneath the stilt-supported cabin and she was getting ready to stand when lightning flashed and the oddly-flat half-light illuminated the surrounding sand dunes. Lee was not a slow learner. She dropped down immediately.

When it was dark again, she wearily pulled herself up. When she reached the base of the wooden steps, he was close behind her. She hesitated for only a moment then shrugged and started up. If his intentions were not honorable, he was surely the most devious rapist imaginable.

The door was open. She hadn't closed it when she had started after the books. And she hadn't closed the French windows from the balcony when she had dashed down from the widow's walk. She ran across the room to shut them, wondering with sharp distress if the rain had ruined anything of value to Mary Margaret.

He came right after her.

"I didn't shut them when I came down from the widow's walk. I thought I would hurry to the car and be right back."

He touched her arm. "Widow's walk?"

She described the square, pavilion-roofed, plank-seated

lookout, and when he understood, he opened the French doors and stepped out into the balcony. “Don't turn on the lights,” he cautioned and he was gone.

She hesitated for an instant, then followed him.

Roofed the loft might be, open air it certainly was. The rain didn't seem to be pelting down quite as viciously as when they crawled across the sand but it still slanted down and swept through the widow's walk.

He seemed oblivious to the rain. He leaned forward, his hands gripping the wooden railing, and slowly turned his head, and she knew his eyes strained to penetrate the wet curtain of the night.

She looked, too, but concentrate though she might, the night seemed a jumble of indistinguishable mounds and lumps. As far as she was concerned, the indomitable six hundred could be marching forward into the jaws, etc., and she wouldn't see a glimmer of it. She gave up trying to divine the enemy's presence and instead looked at the man beside her. Not, of course, that she could really see him. But she could sense him, big and solid and close. It was odd to find that nearness comforting.

Suddenly the world came clear in the half light of lightning. Briefly the surging water foamed onto the grayish beach, the sand dunes rose and fell, and the grasses, flattened by the beat of the rain, glistened.

Dan searched rapidly. He stared the whole way around the cabin. As darkness closed down again, he said flatly, “He's gone.” He turned then and hurried down the steps. Once again she followed. As she closed the French windows, he was already across the room and turning on the light.

He looked down at the telephone. He reached out a blunt strong hand, then pulled it back and jammed both hands in his pants pockets. He stood, head bent, face scowling. His auburn hair clung sleekly to his head like a seal's fur and his thick mustache hung in wet curves.

He realized suddenly that she was watching him. The scowl shifted and fled. For an instant his eyes reflected a swift and approving appraisal of her and she was suddenly conscious of her wet and clinging clothes.

"Look," he said abruptly, "You've been very . . ." He hesitated and she felt a wry flicker of amusement, wondering what word he would choose. Decent, helpful, kind, understanding? There scarcely seemed an appropriate one.

". . . patient. I know you wonder what the hell's happened to your evening but I'm hoping you'll help me some more."

"Do you want to call the police?"

He shook his head.

She realized he was absorbed in working out a thought. "Not yet. I think I'd better see about the girl first. If you'll come with me, perhaps she won't be so frightened."

Lee stared at him.

He looked back and said impatiently, "I know it doesn't make any sense to you. But I'll explain. You will help me, won't you?"

CHAPTER 11

Port Aransas is a little fishing village, the kind of town where the washateria has a community calendar hanging by the telephone. Each day on the calendar carries the names of townspeople celebrating their birthdays. Longtime residents know one another. Most never think about locking a door when they are at home or in their shops.

Evelyn Abbot opened the back door of her shop Saturday night. Once inside, the door closed, she never thought about locking it. She hadn't planned to come back to the shop Saturday night but she felt restless. Normally she read in the evenings. Tonight she wasn't able to get absorbed in a book. The memory of Johnny's scared young face made the graceful sentences in the book meaningless. She'd sighed and put the book down, her mind worrying at how she could help Johnny. She'd told Johnny to bring her a written account of the past few days, quite as if he were a pupil again and she a teacher. It wasn't, perhaps, a bad idea. It might even be a good one, but recalling the week wouldn't save him. It was going to take more than one old teacher's order and a boy's eager response to solve this problem. She'd given an order: Write a paper. She knew the task made Johnny feel better, safer. He hurried off to do her bidding, but likely the information wouldn't provide an answer unless she was very perceptive indeed.

This Saturday evening, she did not feel perceptive. She felt very tired. Her right shoulder was beginning to ache, the bursitis that always warned of weather to come. The rain wasn't far away. She rubbed the aching shoulder and sighed. When she began to wander restlessly around her small living room, she decided to go back to the shop. There is always work to do in your own shop, invoices to be made, letters to write and answer, repairs to plan. There are a thousand-and-one tasks for a shop owner, and a busy mind can't worry. Evelyn learned that a long time ago. Work calms and soothes. It can also console.

So she'd dressed again, changing from her comfortable housecoat to a rose-colored lightly woven knit. She wore low white heels, and, of course, stockings, because she belonged to an older day, a more formal day. She never questioned how she dressed. It was the only comfortable way to dress because, to her, clothing signaled intention. She was going to her shop to work. She was proud of her store and her work and sloppy clothes would have been an offense.

She'd driven unhurriedly to the shop and smelled the coming rain in the air. Once inside, she settled down to work. The fatigue and worry bred of uncertainty in how best to help Johnny began to fade. A little pile of invoices took form beside her typewriter and she hummed softly, "I'm Forever Blowing Bubbles." When the invoices were done, she rested for a moment, brewing a cup of tea on the hotplate in the back of the shop. She carried the cup to her worktable and set out everything she needed to rebind the volume of the Youth's Companion.

She stood at the table to work. The overhead light, a fluorescent fixture, ran the length of the table and it spread a bright pool of shiny light across the back of the shop. She turned on the light in the back room when she came in but she hadn't flicked the switches for the front of the shop. Even so, light spread the length of the shop and gleamed palely through the multi-paned front window. The shade was drawn down on the front door, and a small sign hung from the knob, SORRY, WE'RE CLOSED, but light shone through the windows on either side of the door.

When the rain struck, Evelyn was halfway through with her repairs to the oversized volume. She raised her head to listen for a moment to the rattle of the raindrops on the peaked roof, then bent again to her work. She would have been finished but she became absorbed in the Nature and Science Column and read instead of worked.

It was still raining, but not as fiercely when a knock sounded at the front. The rain was pattering on the roof now, a gentle steady summer rain.

Evelyn looked toward the door. She saw the darkness of a form beyond the shaded front door. She glanced down at her watch. Five minutes to ten. Not so very late, of course. The knock sounded again so she walked toward the front of the shop.

Perhaps it was Johnny. Perhaps he'd thought of something more, something to help them find their way past the ugliness of that hidden package. Perhaps it was that nice girl Lee Porter.

Evelyn Abbott moved slowly. It had been a long day. So many long days any more. She would be fifty-two next month. Not old, certainly, but not young either. She didn't hurry. She walked with her usual dignity. Even when tired, her shoulders didn't sag, her feet didn't drag. It only took a little more effort.

At the door, she reached unhesitatingly for the knob, twisting it, opening the spring lock. She didn't think to step to one side and peer through a square of windowpane to see if a stranger stood on the verandah. Fear was not a part of Port Aransas. Strangers were to be made welcome.

She pulled the door in and looked up at a big young man whose drenched clothes clung to him. She looked beyond him toward the street. Had his car broken down and he needed to call someone? But she saw no car. She stared up at the young man and something in the taut way he stood frightened her.

"What's wrong?" she demanded sharply, her voice thin and high.

His shoulders drew in a little. He leaned closer to her and she could see the wiry thickness of his blond hair and the whites of his eyes and an angry scratch on the side of his face. "Nothing's wrong," he answered his own voice sharp. Then, as if with great effort, he took a deep breath and said, "You the shop lady?" and his hand spread to indicate all the many things displayed.

Her heart pounded in her chest. When she had seen him, huge in the darkness, leaning forward she had been sure it was bad news of some sort. Something had happened to her brother Elliot in San Antonio. Or a fishing boat was past due. Or Johnny's father had been in an accident.

Now she stood and thought herself a silly old woman, her heart beat steadying from a misfortune that hadn't happened. Grateful that there was no bad news, she didn't think to wonder what had generated her fear. She hurried to make amends for her sharp voice, not wishing to be thought rude. "Yes," she said quickly, "I'm Miss Abbott."

"Could I talk to you for a minute?" His voice didn't press. He was a stranger, but his tone was not alien. He spoke in the soft high slow voice of a Texan.

She hesitated. "I'm closed."

"It will only take a minute." There was a plea in his voice.

What would it hurt, she thought, to give him a minute. After all, she was here at the shop. Probably it would turn out that this wasn't quite the sort of shop he had in mind because he certainly didn't look like an antiquary. She smiled. "Of course. Please do come in."

Harry stepped inside. His light blue eyes swept back and forth across the long room then he moved to his left toward the shelving midway down the room. A sign on the counter read: FIRST SHELF—GENUINE ARTIFACTS; SECOND SHELF—REPRODUCTIONS.

He stopped in front of the counter and seemed to search the shelves. His eyes flickered over her collection of pottery figurines from Jalisco and she knew immediately that he was not a true scholar of Mexican art. The figurines were authentic and terribly valuable and she did not ever intend to sell them. In fact, in her will she had made provision for their gift to the University of Texas. She was very proud of them. She had found them many years ago on a buying trip to Mexico. She had bought them for forty pesos, five dollars American at that time, at a little secondhand shop in the District and hadn't discovered their authenticity until years later. She had been offered a fabulous sum for the set by a Dallas banker. Enough money to retire permanently to the Riviera. But she didn't want to leave her sandy little island and she didn't want to part with her figurines.

But the big young man, intent as he was on the case of Mexican artifacts, didn't even spare a glance for the figurines.

She watched curiously. What could he be looking for?

He frowned and rubbed at his temple in the age-old gesture of someone suffering from a headache. His light blue eyes moved again over the collection more slowly this time, from the pottery fragments and the figurines of pre-Columbian days to the intricately carved wooden crucifix of colonial times to the shelf of brightly new but authentic copies, a woven shawl in a mixed pattern, a carved and painted conch shell like those an Aztec priest might have worn, the re-creation of Mayan jade art.

He stood solidly in front of the display case and stared down, his heavy face creased in thought. Water dripped from his sodden clothes and pooled on the shiny yellow wooden floor.

He pointed to the top shelf in the case. "That stuff's all real? I mean, it's really old stuff?"

She nodded, her face polite, but her mind amused at this incredible beginning. This would teach her to let big young men to the shop after closing hours. What could he possibly have in mind?

"Some of it is quite old," she said briskly "The figurines, those statuettes in the center, are at least 1,500 years old."

He nodded in satisfaction. "Yeah, that stuff. Where do you get it?"

Evelyn truly didn't know how to answer that question because there was no single way a dealer obtains goods. Estate sales, smaller shops, private collections, all of these serve as sources.

Impatiently, he asked "I mean, do you buy things like that from some guy in Mexico, some dealer there?"

Sometimes she did. Evelyn nodded. "I have found some things in that fashion. Now, however, there are quite strict limits upon what antiquities can be exported from Mexico. You likely are aware that it is impossible to obtain artifacts which have just been excavated. To obtain something truly old, it's necessary to find something that's been in the market for a long time which, although recognized to be genuine, is not linked to a specific excavation."

She realized he wasn't listening. In fact, he scarcely waited for her explanation to end before he demanded eagerly, hungrily, "What's the name of the man you get things from?"

At her look of utter surprise, he frowned. "I need the name of the man who has old stuff. Somebody who might want some things I know about." He seemed to speak carefully. "I know somebody who has some old stuff." He rubbed his temple again and said ingratiatingly, “My aunt’s got some stuff, some old stuff, to sell and I promised her I’d get the name of some guy in Mexico. She thought it’d be better to sell it down there because the stuff is Mexican.”

“I see,” Evelyn said kindly. “Of course, I’ll be happy to give you his name.”

“And addres[illegible] Harry said quickly.

She looked at him again because she could not mistake the tension in his voice. For some reason it mattered terribly to this young man that she give him this name. Why on earth should it be so important? The name of an antique dealer in Mexico City? Why didn’t he give his aunt’s name? Why didn’t he describe the goods to be sold? Where would such a young man get “old stuff” if not from an aunt?

Theft, of course. But what theft? Where? Evelyn hadn’t read of any recent robberies of art collections. Recent. How recent? Tonight? Her step faltered then with a quick breath she moved ahead. She reached her desk and sat down and drew out a sheet of stationery. As she picked up her fountain pen, she made her decision.

There was something wrong about this young man. What, she couldn’t know. She hoped she didn’t have to learn. But she was not going to give a friend’s name to a predator. She glanced up briefly at the heavy face, the thick blond hair framing it, the dangerous eager face, and knew that he was indeed a predator, violent, quick and deadly.

She drew the paper close and wrote in her clear, beautiful handwriting:

Senor Tomas Herrera
18 Reforma
Mexico, D. F.

She knew no one named Herrera. She finished writing and looked up smiling. "Here you are." She handed the sheet to him. "I don't know what Senor Herrera is buying these days but you can certainly try him."

As the big young man's hand closed tightly on the sheet of paper, Evelyn rose and asked. "Did your aunt send you to me? Would I know her?"

He stared down at her for a long moment, shook his head. "I don't think you'd know her. She lives in Dallas. Walters."

Evelyn was leading the way back toward the front door. "How did you happen to come to my shop?"

His voice relaxed. "I saw the stuff on your window about artifacts and reproductions. I knew you had to get them somewhere so I thought I'd ask."

She nodded but her smile was stiff. The young man lied about so many things. . . . He had no aunt in Dallas. A fool could tell that. And, although one day he must have stood on the verandah and read the lettering on her windows, he had not done it this night. There was no light on the verandah. The only light spread like soft honey from the back of the shop, bright enough to reveal that someone was there but not enough illumination for black lettering on a window.

They were at the front door when she managed to speak again. "It's been very nice talking to you, Mr. . . ."

"Johnson," he said, after a moment.

". . . very nice indeed. I hope you have every success with Senor Herrera."

She was trembling as she closed the front door behind him. She latched it, shoved shut the bolt and sighed with relief as she heard his heavy footsteps going down the verandah steps. Her heart thudded and quivered, a poor frightened thing. What a fool she had been. She would never again answer her door after closing hours.

She turned and walked weakly the long way down the room to her desk. She pulled out her chair and sat heavily in it. She rested for a moment more, then reached for the telephone. She must call the police. She didn't have anything concrete to report but there was something dreadfully wrong about that young man and it would not surprise her to learn that one of Texas most famous collections had been taken. She had been quite lucky that he hadn't sensed her fear.

Her hand still trembled as she checked the directory for the number. She dialed carefully. She heard one ring, then a second, then abruptly, shockingly, terrifyingly, there was no sound at all.

She held the lifeless telephone in her hand for an instant and then she heard, as she had known she would, the soft step in the back room.

CHAPTER 12

Treasure of the Aztecs? That's what he claimed. He seemed rational in the quiet of the beach house despite his bedraggled appearance and she'd heard that crack of a rifle. But was the possibility of ancient treasure any more unlikely, Lee thought, than her presence in an MG hurtling through the rain with a man who'd grabbed her in the darkness and warned her of a killer? The gold of Montezuma. Could this strong-willed, bony-faced man be right?

She studied him in the glow from the dashboard. He hunched over the wheel, his face somber and strained. He hadn't spoken since he finished telling about his day and she knew his mind was ranging ahead, calculating, imagining. She doubted his imaginings were happy ones. He was terribly worried about what might have happened to the girl with the pin. His obvious concern made her decision easy. He wanted her to come with him to reassure the girl. She could do that.

The MG hummed through the quiet streets of Aransas Pass. He slowed as he turned into Nightingale Courts. "She works here. I got the idea she had a room here, too. Maybe the manager can help."

He drove slowly into the parking area. The MG headlights

illuminated a sign by a small wooden house at the back of the lot: Manager. The MG pulled to a stop in front of the structure. He cut the engine.

As he opened his door, Lee said doubtfully, "It's way after eleven o'clock. There's no light in the house. Maybe we should wait until morning." She couldn't see his face clearly. He was half out of the car, pausing in the now gentle rain.

He was brusque. "I've waited too long as it is. I should have stayed with her this morning. I know the value of that kind of find. I should have known she would be in danger. She promised to meet me at nine o'clock tonight. Instead, there was a man with a gun. Where was she? Where is she now?" He pushed away from the car.

She swung out of the car, hurried to catch up. She felt a sharp foreboding. This morning a girl wore a golden pin and walked eagerly down a Corpus Christi street in the summer sunshine. Where was she now?

Dan pulled his key ring from his pocket, used a tiny flashlight to illuminate a bell. He put his finger on the bell, held it. It pealed and pealed and pealed. The windows facing the sidewalk glowed with light. The door stayed shut.

A faint click and Lee knew they were being observed through the peephole in the door.

Dan cleared his throat. "I'm Dan Holloway. This is Miss Porter. We want to see the dark-haired girl who lives here. She was supposed to meet us this evening and she didn't come. It's quite important that we see her."

The little dark circle stayed open. There was the aura of a listening presence but no word was spoken. The door remained shut.

Dan turned his big hands palm up. "It's imperative we talk to her. I'm very much afraid she's in danger."

A long moment passed. Slowly the door opened. A good-sized older woman with carefully blued and tightly curled hair held the front of her dressing gown shut with one hand and gripped the door with the other. Tears glittered in her eyes and she said angrily, "You have a lot of nerve coming here to ask for Judy. As if you don't know where she is! What kind of trick are you trying to play?"

Dan's face folded into a hard frown. "What are you talking about? Do you mean she isn't here now?"

"How could she be?" the woman retorted bitterly. "She hasn't come home since she ran away with you this afternoon. And it won't do her any good to come crawling back now. I told her when she came that I kept a respectable house. There's no place for her here now."

Tears streamed down the old tired face. She slammed shut the door.

Dan pressed the doorbell and kept his finger on it. It buzzed loudly, continuously, a rasping violence in the quiet house.

The door was flung open again.

"You get off my porch or I'll call the police."

"I'm not leaving until you talk to me," Dan replied loudly. "I don't care if I wake up everybody in town or if you call every policeman in Aransas Pass. I'm not leaving until you tell me what you know about Judy because she didn't come with me this afternoon." His voice was grim. "Do you understand me? I haven't seen her since she walked up the sidewalk to this house right at noon."

The older woman stared at Dan.

Lee looked at him, too. His curly reddish hair straggled around his face. His luxuriant handlebar mustache drooped. Now, as midnight neared, a reddish stubble of beard furred his cheeks. His clothes were wet and straggly like his hair. Even in the gloom of the yellowish porch light, the black and purplish bruise on his right cheek was clearly visible and his arms were crisscrossed with scratches and welts. But he didn't look sinister or frightening. He looked worried.

Mrs. Bailey's shoulders slumped. Her face seemed to crumple in on itself. "You don't know where she is?" she asked piteously.

"No," Dan said gently. He continued awkwardly "I'm sorry. I'm very sorry. I hope she is all right, but I'm afraid she's in danger. She's involved in a very dangerous situation. " He tilted his head and looked directly into her eyes. "We have to look for her. Will you talk to us for a moment?"

The manager held the door wide. They stepped into a small living room with too many big pieces of furniture. Lee thought it likely the manager had once lived in a large house. Lee wondered what led her to end her years in a small house on the lot of a motel converted to apartments.

A huge dark-wood secretary loomed to the left. The large overstuffed sofa, the kind known as a chesterfield, was covered in wine-red silk. It would have looked suitable in the captain's cabin of a sailing ship a hundred years ago or in a madam's quarters in New Orleans. Against the wall above the sofa was the portrait of a young man in an ornate round bronze frame. The boy's face was stern, the eyes staring straight ahead, the mouth firm. His khaki shirt bore a sergeant's chevron. His khaki tie was knotted at a young and thin throat. To the right of the portrait in a somber black frame was a small American flag. To the left, another somber black frame squared a small blue flag with a single gold star.

"Sit down, please." She waved them toward the plumped-up pillows of the sofa. She looked tiredly around "Everything's a mess she said unhappily. I wasn't expecting company."

There was no mess. The room smelled of warm stale air and, faintly, of furniture polish and floor wax.

She waited until they sat on the sofa then she took her place on an armless high-backed velvet chair. She sat gingerly on its edge and watched them, her faded brown eyes filled with an expectant dread. "I'm Catherine Bailey. I own the Courts and the café. Judy came to work here a few months ago. What's happened to Judy?"

Dan looked at her intently. "First, I want to understand why you thought Judy was with me."

Mrs. Bailey's plump, work-reddened hands pushed at the sides of her face. "I saw you this morning" she began, "In your car, the little fancy blue car. I saw you talking to Judy and it looked funny to me. She told me later she was giving you directions, but it didn't look right somehow. I thought maybe you were trying to. . . . I mean, it looked like you were saying something to her. Not asking directions."

"Right," he responded. "It was more than directions. It all started this morning in Corpus Christi." He described the way he had first noticed Judy, a girl, a pretty girl, walking down the sidewalk in front of him, how he had come even with her and glanced down and seen a pin that should not have been there.

"That's impossible," Mrs. Bailey said quickly. "Judy couldn't have been wearing a gold pin. She doesn't have any jewelry to speak of, and no money to buy jewels. She doesn't even date any young men, except a few times she went to the movies with Carl Mosley, who lives across the street and he's a ticket taker at the Bijou." The old lady shook her head "Mr. Holloway, you must have been mistaken."

Dan shook his head at that. He told her everything that had happened in Corpus Christi. "I followed her. When I turned in here, she said she was late for work and she couldn't talk. She promised to meet me at nine o'clock at the end of the boardwalk on Mustang Island. She didn't show up. Instead, there was a man with a gun and he was shooting at me."

"Judy wouldn't have anything to do with shooting at you."

"I don't think she would either, but she must have told someone she was going to meet me and why. I think she must have told the man who gave her the pin." He stared somberly at Mrs. Bailey. "He tried to kill me. He must have been determined to keep me from asking Judy about that pin. What does that suggest to you, Mrs. Bailey?"

"I've lived here all my life." There was no disbelief in her voice. "It sounds like treasure. But Judy doesn't know many people. She came to me out of a foster home pretty far inland. She turned eighteen and wanted to see the ocean, that's what she told me. She got enough money together for a bus ticket and came here. She was a good worker. We had such a pleasant time in the evenings after we cleared up at the café. She never said a word about treasure. Why, I can't believe she knew anything about a treasure."

Dan frowned. "Maybe she didn't realize the value of what she had." He nodded to himself. "As a matter of fact, I don't think she knew what she had." He ran his hand through his hair. "So if she told someone I'd stopped her and she was going to meet me tonight, she didn't expect danger." He scowled. "I wish to God I'd stayed here. I should never have driven away."

Lee was puzzled. "Mrs. Bailey, Judy came in to work after you saw her with Dan. But why did you think she'd gone with him when she didn't show up this afternoon?"

"Mr. Cassell saw her get in his car." Mrs. Bailey frowned. "Well, of course, he didn't say it was Mr. Holloway's car. He didn't know anything about you. He just happened to see Judy get into a little blue foreign car."

Dan leaned forward. "Did he say what make of car it was?"

Mrs. Bailey pressed her hands against her temples. "It was at dinner in the café. I said Judy was gone and that probably she'd run away with that man in the little blue foreign car. Mr. Cassell asked what man and I told them how I saw you talking to Judy at noon. Mr. Cassell said he saw her get into a little blue sports car up the street around five o'clock. At least, he said it was a girl who looked like Judy. He said he didn't pay any attention to the man in the car."

Lee felt a chill. A man shot at Dan. And now a man lied and said he saw Judy get into Dan's car. "Who is Mr. Cassell?"

"He has one of the apartments near the back."

Apartments. An old motel room divided into a bedroom and living room with maybe a hot plate wasn't her idea of an apartment. Not her idea of an apartment at all. *Perspiration. Anti-personnel weapons. Passed on.* What was there, Lee wondered, about euphemisms? She was irresistibly reminded of Mencken's acidulous characterization of man's "shoddy and preposterous soul." Then she looked at the older woman, at her weary face and sad eyes, at the dead room with its flags and single portrait and was grateful that Mrs. Bailey hadn't read her thought. Let her use every euphemism in the land if it helped.

Dan leaned forward. "Was Mr. Cassell friendly with Judy?"

"Mr. Cassell isn't friendly with anyone. Some of my renters are quite good friends. Mrs. Frank and the Misses Talbot have such a good time together. Of course he's much younger, [illegible] Cassell is. Keeps very much to himself."

"Younger," Dan repeated. "What age is he?"

"About your age,"

"What does Mr. Cassell do for a living?" Dan asked.

"He's a truck driver for Pan-Con. He often has the run from Corpus to Monterrey."

"Does he have a boat?"

"I think so," Mrs. Bailey answered. "At least, he tracks in lots of sand. That's his only failing, but I say that's little enough to put up with when a man's so regular in paying his rent and no trouble to a soul."

Dan looked grim. "Does he scuba dive?"

The older woman frowned. "Is that when they use those big silver tanks with black hose?"

Dan nodded.

"He has that sort of equipment, but he's never talked about it."

"He must have a boat then," Lee suggested.

"Yes," the older woman said with more certainty, "I believe he does have a boat. The *Lucky Lady*, I think she's called."

Lee looked at Dan. Harry Cassell was likely more than a truck driver or a man who liked the water. He was a treasure hunter with a boat and scuba equipment. Treasure hunter? Treasure finder?

"He told you he saw Judy get into a little blue car," Dan said slowly. "When, Mrs. Bailey? When did he see her?"

"He said it was around five o'clock when he saw her in the car."

"When did you last see her?" Dan asked gently.

"I sent her to the grocery around three."

"Do you know whether she came back from the grocery?" Lee asked.

Yes," Mrs. Bailey said tiredly. "I came here for a little lie-down. I don't ever nap but it was so hot Saturday that I did take a rest. I got to the café at four. The groceries were put away but she hadn't snapped the green beans like I'd asked her."

"You didn't see her after four o'clock?"

Mrs. Bailey shook her head.

"We should talk to Mr. Cassell," Lee said.

"I saw him in the parking lot around nine. He said he was on his way to do some night fishing."

She looked at Dan with wide startled eyes when he said thoughtfully, "Just before nine o'clock. Yes, I want to talk to Cassell. Which is his apartment?"

Mrs. Bailey led the way across the parking lot to the apartment. She knocked. There was silence. She knocked twice more. Nothing sounded beyond the door. Nothing. Mrs. Bailey looked helplessly at Dan.

Dan stepped close to the wooden panel and knocked sharply three times, rattled the knob. "Do you have a key?"

"I can't do that."

In the shadows of the alley, Harry Cassell listened to the rattle of the knob and Mrs. Bailey's sharp protest.

"All right," Dan said grimly. "We'll go to the police."

Harry hurried back to his car. He slid into the driver's seat, turned the motor, drove away. God damn, Harry thought. The police already. He hadn't figured on the police already. How had they gotten on to him so quickly?

He'd driven into the alley after he saw the dark blue MG in front of Mrs. Bailey's house. It was a good thing he kept his eyes open. And it was lucky he'd come back. He'd wanted to pick up a few clothes for his trip. He'd known he was taking a chance but he hadn't figured the man would be after him. He turned out of the alley. Careful, Harry. Don't attract attention. He stopped for the red light and waited impatiently for it to turn. It wouldn't take them long to get the cops, not long at all. He had to get to his tent on Padre. He took SH361, hurtling across Harbor Island toward the ferry to Port Aransas. Nausea burned in his throat. He jammed on the brakes and pulled off on the shoulder. He rubbed at his head. How could he be so stupid? He didn't dare drive down Padre to his campsite. A single road ran down

Mustang and Padre. One road. They could block one road so easy. He didn't dare drive.

Carefully, he swung the car around and headed back toward Aransas Pass. He wasn't going to be trapped.

CHAPTER 13

Lee shivered. It was well past midnight. The policeman had listened politely then asked Judy's age. When they told him, he nodded sagely and said they'd probably get a phone call from Corpus that she was married. Or maybe she'd send a postcard. He wasn't impressed by Mrs. Bailey's claim that she didn't date anybody.

"You'd be surprised," he said patronizingly. "Eighteen and gone from home. It adds up to a boy every time."

The desk sergeant wasn't impressed by exotic tales of an ancient pin and Aztec treasure either. On learning that only Dan had seen the pin and then quite briefly, he tactfully suggested that sometimes things aren't what they seen to be.

Lee demanded sharply how the policeman could account for the fact that Judy was supposed to meet Dan and instead someone shot at him.

The policeman sat up straight at that and pulled his notepad closer, asked quick sharp questions. He stopped writing down the answers after a while. Like the pin, only Dan heard the shots. Only Dan.

Clearly, the policeman thought, this guy was some kind of nut—or maybe he had an axe to grind.

Now his eyes were suspicious, his questions probing. Who was Dan? An archeologist, huh? How long had he been here? How long had he known the young lady here, Miss Porter? Uh-huh. And yeah. The policeman had been quite uninterested in Mr. Cassell. It was some kind of crime to go fishing?

It hadn't been a fruitful discussion as her department chairman was wont to say when his colleagues disagreed with him. It had in fact, been a damn disaster. At one point, Lee wouldn't have been surprised if the sergeant had jailed them on general suspicion of loitering with intent and conspiracy.

The trip to the police station did have one effect. The sergeant's general sense that something smelled funny resulted in the information on Judy's disappearance and the circumstances of its report clattering across the state on the teletype.

They took a silent and exhausted Mrs. Bailey back to her guest house. It was close to one a.m. then. Lee waited in the car while Dan made one last check to see if the elusive Mr. Cassell was in his apartment. Lee realized she was exhausted. It seemed a lifetime ago that she had sat cross-legged in the sunshine and sketched a boat named the *Sue Belle* II. She wasn't surprised when Dan returned to the car, shaking his head. She had not really expected Mr. Cassell to be back.

There wasn't much to say on the drive back to Port Aransas. Dan was somber, abstracted. He did rouse, as they sat waiting for the ferry, to say, "I appreciate your coming with me tonight. I've put you to a lot of trouble."

"That's all right," she said awkwardly because it would have been patently phony to say he hadn't caused her any trouble. "I'm sorry it didn't turn out better." She paused. "I hope the girl is all right."

"If I hadn't tried to stop her she would have been fine."

Lee surprised herself at the sharpness of her rebuke. "Don't blame yourself. If you hadn't noticed the pin, someone else would have. Once she wore the pin, she was lost."

"Maybe," was all he said, but she knew he found some comfort in her words.

When the little car pulled up near the beach house, he insisted on coming inside and checking. Just in case, he said. Then, his face lined with weariness, he thanked her again and left.

It was almost two in the morning then. The rain had stopped almost an hour before but it was a steamy muggy night. She washed her face, pulled on a shorty nightgown and tumbled down into sleep. She slept heavily, unmoving, not even waking to close the windows when the temperature began to drop.

It was the cold which wakened her finally, wakened her to a puzzling grayness. For a moment, she felt lost, the room unfamiliar, time all askew. She pulled the sheet tightly around her then, still cold, reached down for the spread at the foot of the bed but even that wasn't enough. She lay there shivering but awake and turned her face to look at the clock then tossed back the covers and jumped out of bed. Fifteen minutes to nine and she had promised to meet Miss Abbott and Johnny at nine.

Lee shook her head as she drove hurriedly up 11th Street on the misty Sunday morning. She was late before she started. The sky was somber, thick black clouds warning of more rain to come. As she neared the channel, she heard fog horns, a lonely sound, like the eerie call of a train whistle just before dawn.

She turned left onto Cotter and pulled into a parking place in front of the building. She was closing the door of the VW when she paused and frowned. There was no welcoming light in the shop window. She stared, at dark windows and for an instant felt rebuffed, unwanted. Surely Miss Abbott was here. The time had been set. She was the kind of person who kept commitments. If she cited a time, made an appointment, she would do as she'd promised.

As Lee started up the wide steps, she heard steps on the verandah. She looked up expectantly and waved at Johnny.

He reached the front door, waited for her. He was frowning. He called out, "I tried the door and it's locked."

She joined him. "Do you suppose she's late?"

"I guess so. But she said nine o'clock." He looked at his watch. "It's almost nine-twenty." Worry was clear in his voice.

Lee felt uncertain. "She'll probably be here any minute."

"She's never late." Johnny rattled the knob again.

"Everybody's late sometimes," Lee said gently. She saw pages of tablet paper clutched in his right hand. "I see you put together some information."

He nodded uncomfortably, poked the pages toward her. "Would you like to read it?"

"Of course."

She took the somewhat limp sheets. Johnny had divided his report into days, starting with the previous Monday. Lee scanned the painstaking recital of what he had done and when and what he had said and what had been said to him.

He and his father had a charter parties Monday and Tuesday. Lee skimmed over the men's names. It was Tuesday night that the call came of his aunt's death. His father left Wednesday morning for Missouri. Wednesday there had been no charter. Lee read more carefully the rounded painstakingly written words, sensing a suddenly defensive turn of phrase.

". . . we didn't have a charter scheduled Wednesday so I worked around, cleaning up. I put in some new spark plugs and since I wanted to give them a try, see how the motor sounded, I took the *Sue Belle* out for a cruise. And it's good practice to see if you plotted a good fix and I had one from Tuesday on the chart that I wanted to check out. Turned out I was right on the dot. It was a motor boat that we passed on Monday and Tuesday, same place both times. There was a girl and she was real friendly Tuesday, so when I was out there Wednesday I stopped to talk for a minute. It was kind of funny because she was fishing and it looked like she was all by herself, but when I asked she said she wasn't alone. Then, she looked kind of worried. There wasn't a diver's flag around anywhere and I couldn't see anybody else on the boat and I could see right into the cabin. Then there was a kind of hollow thump and she looked real scared and told me to go. I guess somebody was diving and not using a flag. That's dumb. Anyway, I went on like she asked me to. Thursday I cleaned out all the lockers and that's how I know the stuff wasn't in. . . ."

Lee's eyes skimmed back up the page to the boat and the girl who looked like she was alone but said she wasn't. No diver's flag. Dan thought the gold, the precious bit of gold, was surely salvage from a newly found galleon. He said only a galleon carried such treasure.

She gripped Johnny's arm. "What did the girl on the motor boat look like?"

He shrugged his shoulders. "She was pretty cute."

"Was she a blonde?"

"No, she had black hair, real pretty black hair, all thick and curly. And she had a good tan and she had on a swell swim suit."

Lee could have smiled at that. A swell swim suit was one way of saying a girl was stacked. But if the girl had been Judy, there was no time to smile.

"How old was she. Johnny?"

"My age. Seventeen, eighteen."

Lee looked back down at the lined paper and the rounded

words and could almost see a plump face, a young body. The girl was Judy. Lee was suddenly as sure of that as she had ever been sure of anything. Judy, smiling at Johnny, Judy, hurrying down the street in sunshiny Corpus Christi, a small golden pin on her blouse.

Lee said urgently, "If the girl on the boat is who I think she is, all of this ties into something else, something very serious." She remembered the shots that crackled through the night at Dan. Anybody who would shoot a man to keep a treasure secret certainly wouldn't balk at planting cocaine on somebody's boat. "Did you go back to this same spot on Thursday?" Lee asked sharply.

His face reddened. "Yeah. I happened to be out that way."

Yeah, she thought, he just happened to be out that way. She wasn't too clear upon how one progressed to what seemed to her the limitless expanse of the Gulf, but she felt sure one did not just casually happen anywhere. Lee balanced the information in her mind. What if the girl was Judy and the man this elusive Mr. Cassell and what if Mr. Cassell was busily scooping up millions in treasure from the sea bottom, what then would be Mr. Cassell's response to a boat that came by too many times?

Somebody shot at Dan because he tried to trace a pin. What would that somebody do to someone who snooped right above the golden hoard?

"Did you see the girl again?"

Johnny looked down at the wooden verandah. "Yeah. She wouldn't even look at the *Sue Belle*."

So the boy had gone by the motor boat four days running.

"Johnny, I want you to come with me and meet a man who may know something about all this. He's an archeologist and he thinks someone has found another of the silver fleet galleons and the girl you saw may have been mixed up in it. The fact that you saw her may be what made someone try to get you jailed." Lee tugged at his sleeve.

He stood unmoving. "Miss Abbott said nine o'clock. Now it's almost ten. I can't go off. I have to wait for Miss Abbott."

Lee stopped tugging on his sleeve and tried to persuade. She explained how she had reasoned it out. If Johnny and Dan decided between them that the girl in the boat was Judy, that could explain why someone—Cassell—put cocaine on the *Sue Belle*. Johnny could be exonerated.

Johnny listened. He understood but he still wasn't leaving. "You go get this fellow and I'll talk to him. But I'm not leaving until Miss Abbott comes." He looked determined, immovable.

Lee glanced at her watch. Johnny was right. It was almost ten. And that was odd. Suddenly she too was worried. "Let's check in back," Lee said abruptly. "Maybe she didn't hear us knock."

He didn't answer but turned on his heel and walked swiftly down the verandah toward the end of the building. She knew he recognized the feebleness of her excuse. Miss Abbott would not sit at the back of her shop for an hour past the time she expected company. She would certainly have heard Johnny's forceful knock.

Lee ran to keep up with Johnny as he hurried along the side of the building. She was right behind him when he stopped abruptly at the end of the building and said, "Her car." His voice was high.

Lee moved past him and led the way up the wooden steps to the back door. She didn't knock. She grabbed the knob. The knob turned and the door opened. Her throat closed with fear of what might be inside.

"Hurry up." Johnny pressed close behind her.

She forced herself to step inside although she was afraid, terribly afraid, of what they might find.

The light was on in the back room. That confirmed her worst

fears. Miss Abbott would not go off and leave a light burning. Hesitantly, she moved forward and looked carefully around. She saw bins and shelves filled mostly with items to be repaired. Cartons and boxes ranged alongside one wall in an orderly fashion. Nowhere did Lee see Miss Abbott.

She moved forward. The door to the main showroom was closed. Lee walked up to it, took a deep breath and pulled it open. At first glance nothing seemed out of order. She hurried to the middle of the room and looked up and down the rows of tables and, finally, felt an overwhelming sense of relief. Wherever Miss Abbott was, she was not in this room. Not in this shop.

Perhaps, Lee hoped, there was some simple explanation for the car parked outside. Perhaps it wouldn't start and a friend picked her up and took her home and she hadn't been able to come in yet this morning and she would walk through the door in only a moment more and smile and shake her head at her carelessness in having left the back door unlocked.

The lights were on above the worktable. Slowly she walked to the table and looked down. Lee sighed. *E. Abbott, Prop. And Artist* would not leave a job half done. She would not walk away and leave a bottle of rubber cement uncapped to the air.

Lee leaned forward and picked up the cap to the glue bottle and gently screwed it onto the bottle. Johnny came striding across the room, his voice loud with relief. "I guess everything's okay. Miss Abbott's not here sick or anything."

Lee held up her hand and the boy stood very still. The tall slim girl stared down at the worktable and slowly shook her head. The volume of the Youth's Companion lay open. Lee saw where Miss Abbott had been working on the spine of the book.

The corner of one page was ripped. The page had not been ripped the morning before. Her gaze locked on thick red underlining near the top of the page. The red marker underlined portions of the drop head to the continuing saga of excitement: In The Clutch of The Tsar.

The headline read:

> Taken to town jail.—Robbed by the soldiers.—Thrust into bad company. A dingy courtroom and a severe sentence. Put with a chain gang.—At a coal mine.—Its terrors, and an unpleasant encounter.

The lead of the red pencil had gouged deeply into the old dry page in the thick line drawn under an unpleasant encounter.

Lee read that very same drop head yesterday morning. There were no penciled red lines.

CHAPTER 14

Once Lee saw those red scrawls on the yellowed page, she looked around the room with searching eyes and other wrong things, each small in itself, clamored for attention. The half-open drawer on the left side of Miss Abbott's desk. The telephone handset out of its cradle. Lee stared at the telephone. She reached out and picked up the receiver, listened. No dial tone, as silent as a tomb. No signal buzzed an irascible warning.

Looking again at the worktable, Lee saw the shiny lacquered finish of a straw handbag. On its front, sea shells curved to form a jumping porpoise. The purse was not an antique. It was new and fashionable. Lee picked it up and opened it.

She looked inside, hating to pry but knowing she must. A woman's handbag is a very personal thing, a very private thing. Lee saw a lace-edged handkerchief, a small cut glass vial of cologne, a lipstick, a sack of ice mints, a change purse, and a soft leather wallet. She picked up the wallet. The driver's license was made out to Evelyn Abbot, single, female, age 52, height 5 feet 3 inches, weight 134, hair brown, eyes blue, no distinguishing marks.

Lee dropped the wallet back into the purse and looked

somberly at Johnny. Lee did not know which frightened her the most, the purse or the dead telephone.

Johnny called from the back of the room. "Somebody pulled out the telephone wires."

She came and looked down at sagging black wire and then at the purse which she still held in her hand. No woman leaves her purse behind willingly.

Lee and Johnny didn't even take time to get the VW. They ran, Johnny in the lead, the half-block down Cotter Road to the small, one-story City Hall which housed the Port Aransas police.

Lee didn't stop to think that it was Sunday and to wonder whether the station would be closed. It didn't occur to her to wonder why it was open when she and Johnny turned the knob and clattered into the front office.

Every light burned. The dispatcher sat tensely at his console. "Right. See what you can dig up on her and get back to us as soon as possible. We've sent the body to the M.E.'s office in Corpus and we'll deal with the sheriff there. Right. We'll be back in touch with you."

The dispatcher looked around at Lee and Johnny by the front counter. "Unless it's an emergency I'll have to ask you to come back later."

"It is an emergency," Johnny said quickly. "Miss Abbott is missing."

The husky young man frowned then got up and came to the counter.

"Miss Abbott at the antique shop?"

"Yes," Johnny replied. "Can we talk to the chief? We're afraid something's happened to her."

The young policeman shook his head. "I don't think you can right now. We've had some bad stuff. A girl's been murdered and the chief's questioning the guy who probably did it."

Automatically, Lee and Johnny looked at the closed door marked *CHIEF OF POLICE, ARANSAS PASS.*

"Who got killed?" Johnny asked.

The policeman looked uncertain then said, "Well, it's not out yet but we think it's a girl who was reported missing from Aransas Pass. And it looks pretty much like we've got the guy who did it."

"What is the girl's name?" Lee asked in a thin voice.

"Judy Martin. Just a kid." The young policeman shook his head. "Goddam, you'd think girls would learn to stay away from men they don't know."

Lee was starting to ask him the name of the suspect when the door to the chief's office opened.

Dan stood in the doorway, head up, his thick auburn hair curling tightly in the damp weather, his heavy red mustache drooping. He looked back into the office. His voice was tough. "No, Chief it's your turn to listen to me. You've got a murder, yes, but you don't have your murderer. Hell, I was the one who reported her missing, You find my name on the report so you push your way into my motel room and haul me down here and accuse me of murder and kidnapping and second-degree rape and you don't listen to a word I say."

Dan took a deep breath. "I've answered your questions as long as I'm going to. I'm walking out of here and you can't stop me unless you charge me with murder in which case I want a lawyer."

It was silent for a moment.

Some of the anger seeped out of Dan. He shook his head tiredly. "If you'll pay some attention to what I've told you, you'll start hunting for the man who has found himself a treasure galleon."

The voice from the office was harsh. "Nobody saw a pin but you."

Dan shrugged. "I can't help you if you won't listen." He turned to come out into the front office.

"Mr. Holloway."

Dan swung on his heel and glared. "I'm leaving or you're charging me. Make up your mind."

A chair scraped. Deliberate footsteps sounded on asphalt tile flooring.

Lee craned her neck to see beyond Dan.

The police chief was a much smaller man. He stood perhaps five feet six to Dan's five eleven. He was older. His faded blond hair was thinning and lay in separate lank strips on his head. He was thin and his weathered skin drooped in folds and furrows on his reddish face. But he faced Dan with dignity.

"You think you can have everything your way because you're somebody. Because you're Dr. Daniel Holloway. I'll tell you something, doctor. You may be somebody but I don't care how big you are, I'll get you if you killed that little girl."

Before Dan could respond the smaller man continued "But by the same token, I ain't trying to make it look like a man's guilty if he isn't. So, if you'll agree, I'll keep your car and run some tests on it and I'll have my men out asking about the girl and about that pin."

"That's fair enough," Dan said. He hesitated then added, "Have them ask about Harry Cassell."

The chief slowly nodded. "All right, sir, I will."

"I'm free to go then?" Dan asked.

"Right," the chief said. "All I'm asking is that you don't leave the area."

Johnny broke in impatiently, "Chief!"

Dan and the chief both looked out and Dan saw Lee.

"Chief Lingren," Johnny said urgently, "Listen. Something's happened to Miss Abbott. She's disappeared."

The chief brushed past Dan and hurried to Johnny. "What's happened, son? Has her house been broken into? The shop?"

"It's the shop," Johnny replied. "Miss Abbott was supposed to meet me and Miss Porter at the shop at nine this morning. Miss Abbott wanted me to think about everything that had happened so we could figure out who hid the cocaine on the *Sue Belle*. You know about the . . ." At the chief's impatient nod, Johnny continued, "Anyway, Miss Abbott said she'd be there at nine o'clock. I got there at nine and nobody was there. About nine thirty, Miss Porter came and we knocked again. No answer. Miss Porter reads the stuff I've written down and then she wants me to come and talk to some guy about whether a girl I saw is the same one this guy's hunting for. I think maybe it was Dr. Holloway she wanted me to talk to but I said I wouldn't leave 'til Miss Abbott comes. So then it's ten o'clock and we really get worried so we went around to the back and Miss Abbott's car is there. The back door's unlocked and we go inside and we find a light on and the telephone wire pulled out from the wall."

"Her purse was there on the worktable," Lee said.

The chief frowned. "What did you find at her house?"

Johnny looked blank.

"We didn't try her house," Lee said impatiently. "It's obvious that something happened at the shop."

The chief shoved a hand through his thinning hair. "How in the world can you come here and raise a hue and cry when you haven't even checked to see if she's at home?" He turned away and crossed to a nearby desk and picked up the telephone receiver. He flipped open the directory found the number and dialed. He dialed as if the telephone were an enemy, stubbing his finger into the slot and yanking the dial around.

Everyone waited when he finished dialing. He held the phone

to his ear for a long time. Fifteen rings at least. In the quiet of the office, everyone could hear the shrill of the telephone bell as he slowly replaced the receiver in the cradle.

He turned his head to look at Lee and Johnny. "You say the back door of the shop was unlocked?"

They nodded.

"Anything broken up? Any vandalism? Any signs of a struggle?"

"Just the telephone wire pulled loose," Johnny said slowly.

The chief frowned. "The back door was shut, wasn't it?"

Johnny nodded.

"Well, then," the sheriff said more easily, "she might just have forgotten to lock it."

Lee started to speak then kept quiet. After all, just because she happened to live in a fairly tough neighborhood near her urban college and would never in a thousand years forget to lock a door, didn't mean she could cite the absurdity of an unlocked door on Miss Abbott's behalf.

"And the wires," the chief continued quickly, "maybe they were pulled loose accidentally. She could have been moving something." The chief shrugged then asked, "Where's your purse, Miss Porter?"

Lee wished fervently for a women's lib placard. She would happily have smashed it over his head. "I'm not carrying a purse this morning. I tucked my billfold in my jacket pocket. But Miss Abbott isn't the kind of woman who goes out without her purse. Besides, her billfold's in her purse. I looked."

The chief shrugged again. "Something may have called her away in a hurry."

Lee shook her head hopelessly, then suddenly her eyes widened. She had proof, proof positive. "Please," she said eagerly, "I know something bad happened to Miss Abbott and I can prove it."

The words tumbled over one another as she described the volume of collected papers, how she and Miss Abbott had looked at them together and laughed about the old-fashioned tale of drama that was yet so clearly a brother to the modern suspense novel. How Miss Abbott had prized the worn volume. How there had been no red lines drawn under those suggestive sentences:

Thrust into bad company. An unpleasant encounter.

"Don't you see? Someone came and forced her to leave."

The chief couldn't quite hide a smile. "But he let her mark up a message with a red pencil first. I'm sorry, miss. I guess I'm just a country boy but I think you and Johnny have kind of lost your heads." He paused and looked down at his watch and the smile slipped off his face.

The two-way radio gave a warning buzz. The chief looked at it, then at them. He was brusque now, "I've got more on my plate right now than I can handle. We're just a three-man force. I've called on Aransas Pass and the county to help us with this murder. I don't have time for any foolishness right now. I know Evelyn Abbott and she's a sensible lady. She can take care of herself so you folks don't need to waste your time and mine worrying about her."

CHAPTER 15

Evelyn Abbott lay quietly and stared at the small gray triangle of the tent opening. How long had the dangerous young man been gone? Hours and hours and hours. Had he left her here to die? No. His treasure was here. He would at all costs come back for his treasure. What would happen to her when he returned?

Last night he moved so quietly from the storeroom into the showroom. He held his hands out in front of him, spread wide and there had been a feral quality in the movement of his body.

She watched him approach, wordless, unmoving. Perhaps her quietness saved her. She made no effort to stand and run, try to escape. She was no match for his strength. When the phone went dead and she heard that soft step, she knew he'd returned. In that instant, she picked up the red pencil and marked those melodramatic lines. She marked them without much hope but she carried a memory of Lee's clear gray eyes. Intelligent eyes. Noticing eyes. It wasn't much to build on but it was something. Then she turned her chair to face the doorway to the back room. The red pencil slipped soundlessly onto the table as he walked toward her.

"Who were you trying to call?" His voice was too high, too soft.

She said nothing.

He stopped in front of her. He rubbed at his temple. "Do you speak Spanish?"

For a moment she thought her mind had gone, but the question hung in the air. She hurried to answer as a frown gathered on his face. "Yes. I speak Spanish quite well." A life can hang on such little things. Now children, say after me, "Buenas noches, senores, buenas tardes, senorita, como esta usted?" How many years ago had she sat in a hard straight chair and parroted those phrases?

He nodded. "You come with me then. I got things to sell in Mexico. You come with me and help me sell them." He rubbed his head again and said almost as if to himself, "If anybody tries to stop me, I'll tell them I've got you."

A hostage, she thought. But that was better than it could be. She wouldn't make a very useful hostage dead. For the first time since he moved so quietly toward her, she began to believe in a future.

He walked to her desk and opened the drawers, one after another. She said nothing when he lifted out the .45. Her brother Elliott had given it to her. He had insisted. A woman alone ought to have a gun. Now the gun was where guns so often ended up, in the hands of a dangerous man.

She went with him without protest. She left her purse behind. Another small hope. He hadn't noticed. Young men know so little about women.

Pendants, bracelets, breast plates, face masks, labrets, rings, necklaces. Evelyn marveled at his descriptions. Clearly, he had no understanding of the value of what he had found. He knew gold was worth money, that he knew. But that he held in his hands the artistic triumphs of a people, Aztec gold-work when its civilization was pulsing with vitality, this he didn't know and likely wouldn't understand. But he knew there was money to be had, money that he felt belonged to him.

She listened and occasionally asked a mild question. How had he cleaned the jewels? Had they been heavily crusted with barnacles? At what depth beneath the sand had he found them?

She was too nearsighted to make out the numbers clicking steadily on the dimly lit odometer, but they drove past the ranger station and the entrance to Malaquite Beach. It wasn't much longer until they turned off onto a beach access road. When the old car reached the beach and drove along the hard-packed sand, Evelyn knew she had never seen a lonelier, blacker night. The headlights penetrated the darkness and the rain only far enough to show the sand stretching out before them. They passed no car, no tent, no one.

He checked the odometer more and more often, then braked the car to a stop. He picked up a flashlight from the front seat floor. "Come on."

So far he hadn't hurt her when she did as she was told. She climbed out of the car and followed. They walked, rain slapping down on them, toward the dunes. The light of the flashlight didn't pierce far enough to show the dunes but that was the direction he took. Gradually the sand softened and deepened and abruptly they were into the dunes.

She concentrated on stepping as nearly as possible on clumps of dun grass briefly revealed by the dancing light.

He seemed to find his way without difficulty then. Every

twenty feet or so he swung the flashlight beam about until the beam settled on a neat pile of beer cans or an empty gasoline tin or an arranged stack of driftwood. Signposts along the way to somewhere. They walked for almost half an hour, up dune and down. Evelyn fell and pulled herself up and staggered on until her world was a nightmare of cold rain and shifting sand and bone jolting missteps. She forgot everything but the necessity of putting one foot in front of the other so she stumbled into him when he stopped in a gully.

He pointed the flashlight to the right. She stared at the dune, puzzled. Then she saw the misshapen bulge in the downward slope.

He was very proud of the dun-colored tent rigged on the slope. It looked like part of the sand. He showed her how had had shored the ever-shifting face of the dune with old timbers. In time, the dune would move in its eternal march and bury everything in its path but for now the timbers held fast and the strong canvas tent afforded a three-foot clearance. It was big enough to crawl into. It was big enough to hold part of the treasure of the House of Axayacatl.

She crawled into the tent without a murmur she was so grateful to be at rest.

He lit the Coleman lamp and its cheerful flicker warmed her spirit if not her body.

She looked curiously around. A sleeping bag was rolled up against the back of the tent. Near it sat a metal cooler, a cardboard box, and a toolbox.

He leaned over and opened up the tool box and lifted out a tape measure. He placed one end of the tape flush to the near corner of the cooler and rolled it out straight for about a foot and a half. At that point he began to scoop away sand. It took him a long time to uncover the entire lid of a buried footlocker.

He raised the lid, stared for a few minutes, slowly closed it, and sat back on his heels.

Despite her fatigue she watched him carefully. His heavy face furrowed, his hands clenched. He was thinking. The labor of thought was as obvious and genuine as the rough scratch of the sand and the damp chill of the night air. He thought for a long time. Finally he looked at Evelyn "I have to go get something. You'll have to stay here."

He pulled a coil of rope out of the toolbox. He tied her securely but not unkindly. He stared down at her for a moment then picked up an army blanket and spread it over her.

He extinguished the lamp and took the flashlight, leaving her in absolute darkness. She lay under the heavy wool blanket and was grateful for the slow return of warmth to her chilled body. She drifted into an uneasy, uncomfortable sleep. She woke suddenly, abruptly, and lay stiff and frightened, listening to the wind, the heavier stronger moaning wind. Dunes move. They can move swiftly, obliterating everything in their path. She lay and listened to the rising tempo of the wind. There would be more rain. She had lived on the island for a long time and the sound of the wind was a meaningful sound. There would be hard rain and heavy seas.

Sometimes in hurricane weather, waves sweep all the way across Padre Island.

She didn't sleep again. She lay, her wrists chafed, the bursitis in her right shoulder a continuing pain, her stiff and aching legs a reminder of the trek over the dunes, and waited.

The gray dawn came gradually and the triangular tent opening framed the sodden petals of morning glories and rain-flattened eel grass.

Nothing warned her. No faint roar of a motor, no telltale rustling in the wet dune grass. One moment the patch of dune was visible, the next it was blocked away, hidden by his body as he ducked into the tent.

She knew something had gone wrong even before she saw his pale and strained face. It took no words to tell it. He carried the wildness of a caged leopard in his body. He emanated danger as clearly as a dangling powerline or a broken railing on a roof. Stay clear. Beware.

"We got to go." His voice high and thin. "They already called the cops. I don't know how they knew but it changes everything. I was afraid to bring the car back down, man. It would be easy to get trapped on the island. You know?"

Evelyn nodded.

"I came in my boat. That's what took me so long. I had to wait till it was light so I could find the right place." He stared at her. "Can you swim?"

"Yes."

"You see, we have to get back out to the boat. I anchored. Two anchors. It took me a long time to get it just right. Safe. I came in with a rubber dinghy. We can get back out."

Involuntarily, Evelyn looked toward the tent opening and listened to the hiss of the rain and, even this far from the beach, the crash of the surf.

"We can," he said again.

She knew it didn't matter whether they could. They were going to try.

He lifted up the lid of the footlocker and stared into it then looked worriedly around the tent. He grabbed the tool chest and quickly emptied it then he began to lift towel-wrapped packets from the buried footlocker and she knew that within the protective cotton nestled the gold of Montezuma. He filled the toolbox and shut it and shoved it toward the front of the tent. Then he picked up the ice chest and dumped out water and pieces of ice and a half dozen cans of beer. It didn't take him long. When both containers were ready at the tent opening, he knelt and cut loose her ropes.

"Come on," he said harshly.

Somehow she managed to move her stiffened muscles and crawl out of the tent into the icy wash of wind-driven rain. She managed to follow him though the effort took every ounce of her will and strength. He moved as slowly as she, burdened by the toolbox under his right arm and the ice chest under his left.

The beach was even more daunting in the gray half-light of morning than it was in the night. She was old and tired and even more frightened by the sharp slanting sweep of rain, the lowering sky black, the immense waves.

He tied the toolbox and the ice chest securely in the rubber dinghy. She stood by and watched the waves hurl themselves toward the shore. She had never been afraid of the Gulf. She had always treated the Gulf with respect, never presuming upon her knowledge of the sea. Standing on the rain-swept beach, her knit dress sagging coldly against her, her feet cut and bruised from the shells, aching with cold and exhaustion, she was very much afraid.

He didn't hurry as he tied the chests to the dinghy. He pulled on the ropes, tested them. He doubled the knots. Finally he was satisfied. He stood and stared at the storm-churned sea. The wind was strong enough to make her lean forward.

"There." He pointed out across the water.

She strained to see. Beyond the arching maelstrom of breaking waves, she finally saw a motor boat, straining and pulling against its anchors.

So far his luck had held, she thought dispassionately. That must have been a very tough anchorage and he had done it.

Getting to shore on the dinghy had been no mean feat, either. How far was his luck going to run?

He began to pull the dinghy toward the water. She hesitated for an instant. Could she run away? Hide in the dunes? She looked at the drawn hunch of his shoulders and knew he was beyond patience. If she crossed him, he would kill her. Quickly. Later he might say, "I didn't mean to hurt the old lady. But she should've come. She shouldn't have tried to run away."

She stepped into the swirling shallows. Oddly the water was warmer than the rain. She followed him, watching the oncoming waves. The trick, of course, was to get beyond the breakers. They would still have to battle a steep sea but the worst danger was the surf.

"Now," he yelled and somehow, insanely, she was splashing into the waves after him, holding tight to a rubber oarlock on the side of the raft. He had timed their forward rush well. They pushed against incoming water. The surging water was knee high, waist high, chest high. She clutched the boat with one hand, stroked with the other. They were past the first breaker, the second, the third. The fourth rose ahead, arching higher and higher, flickers of foam quivering at its crest, enormous, horrifying.

She kicked and swam and pushed and heaved with all her strength. There was no time to go back. They must top the wave before thousands of pounds of water smashed down on them. If the monstrous wave broke on them, they would be thrown against the ocean floor with the crushing force of a toppling brick wall.

Up, up, up, she swam willing the dinghy to rise. The foam glistened. If the raft slipped back even a little they were doomed. Then they were at the top and tumbling down into the trough and she felt the wave break behind them.

Another wave loomed hungrily above them but it was not a giantess. They struggled up and over it and they were beyond the breakers.

Their world was compassed by steep-sided seas that blocked the view of anything but the cloud-darkened sky directly above them. She felt an angry despair because they would not be able to see the motor boat. They were trapped by walls of water.

She clung to the raft with both hands now. She couldn't hold on much longer. Her arms ached. Her cheek pressed against the slick side of the raft. She smelled rubber even above the salt of the sea. She hung on and wondered why she did. It was only a matter of minutes, perhaps seconds, and her hands would give way and she would slip down into the roiling water, perhaps to fight to the surface and swim desperately for a few strokes. The end would be the same, a final effort, a final failure. Why didn't she let go now? Did she expect a lightship to come suddenly into view? Did she think a buoy would appear and she could grab it? She was old and tired and rapidly weakening and she had no hope but she would continue to hang on for a minute, for seconds, for any time at all. Defeat was not surrender.

Her eyes closed. Her whole being was intent upon her desperate grip on the oarlock. The noise of the tortured water, the thunder of the surf, the splash of the rain, all receded. There was nothing in the world but her hands and the hard stubby circle of rubber to which they clung.

At first the harsh pressure on her arms was meaningless, a faint incursion into the reality of her battle for survival. Then her grasp on the ring was torn loose but miraculously, she was being pulled up into the raft, not being dragged down into the clutching water.

She opened her eyes as he dumped her unceremoniously on the bottom of the rubber boat.

"Balance," he shouted. "Balance."

She stared at him, wondering what on earth he meant. The little craft dipped down into a trough and she began to slide toward him and she understood. She learned quickly. She watched the waves, leaned this way or that as needed. When the little raft rode on the crest of a wave they could see until the mist and rain closed in. And there, to the right, swung the motor boat on its lines.

The *Lucky Lady* looked huge and sturdy and sea worthy from the vantage point of the rubber raft. She helped balance and forgot her weariness. She had despaired and now all things looked possible.

It was a struggle all the way, to paddle the little raft to the motor boat, to tie up and clamber aboard in a lurching heaving world, to transfer the heavy chests. Once the chests were aboard and securely tied inside the cabin, Harry cast off the raft, hauled in the anchors and got underway.

For a long while, content merely to be out of the pelting rain and not at the mercy of the waves, she sat quietly on the floor of the cabin. She watched him at the wheel, intent, purposeful, and finally she asked, "Where are we going?"

"I got it all worked out," he said softly "I got my keys to the yard. I'll get one of the trucks not due out 'til later in the week. Nobody could possibly miss it until tomorrow at the soonest. Probably not 'til Wednesday or Thursday. We'll be over the border tonight. The border guards know the Pan-Con trucks. They usually just wave us through."

He nodded to himself in satisfaction then lifted his head and stared at the awesome water. "But first," he said determinedly, "I got to go down one more time. Just one more time."

His voice fell away and it seemed to her that the *Lucky Lady* picked up speed, bucking its way into the waves harder and faster.

She knew she had heard correctly, but she asked anyway "Down?"

He looked around at her and she saw the hunger in his eyes. "I was going back down but that helicopter came. I was afraid to stay any longer. But you know what I found?"

Slowly she shook her head.

His voice was soft and excited. "I needed to make a sling for it. It was a big circle all covered with barnacles. A big circle, maybe two feet across. I broke off some of the barnacles. It was a circle of gold."

She looked at him and almost spoke to warn him. You fool, you fool, you have enough. Go and take what you have. But she didn't speak. If he went down, she might have a chance. If he went down in this dreadful storm-tossed water and she was in control of the boat . . .

CHAPTER 16

Lee looked at the mountainous wall of water poised above. This foaming, curling, breaking wave was going to thunder down and swamp the *Sue Belle.* Lee clung to the rail and stared at the pulsating mass of water. She had never seen anything more inimical as the grayish-green, foam-flecked writhing cliff of water hanging above her.

Somehow, surely it was a miracle, the *Sue Belle* sluggishly, heavily, wallowed ahead of hungry, looming waves. The bow dipped down into the water. Lee gripped the railing, stiffened her legs against the dreadful pitch. With agonizing slowness, the *Sue Belle* rose, clawing her way up.

Up and down, each time harder than before. With maddening regularity, the *Sue Belle*'s fog whistle shrilled. If she lived long enough that sound was going to drive her crazy. But, as she looked back over her shoulder at the tons of water beginning to crest, she doubted she would have to hear the mournful cry for all that long a time. But, so far, the *Sue Belle,* like an early silent film heroine snatched from, the gleaming rails at the last possible instant, began to climb.

Over the unearthly rumbling and hissing of the water, Lee heard the sharp crash each time the bow of the *Sue Belle* whacked down into a trough, the agonized jolt of wood upon wood as she creaked. Lee felt sure she would be even more frightened if she knew enough about boats to gauge the stress the *Sue Belle* was bearing.

And for what? The stupidity of their plight infuriated her. Who did Dan Holloway think he was with his arrogant assumption of command? She was equally angry at herself. Why did she consent to come? She was under no compulsion to follow orders from Dan Holloway.

The *Sue Belle* tilted into a trough, slammed down, wobbled, slowly righted herself. Now the boat not only plunged down and clambered up, but lurched heavily from side to side, all in one sickening corkscrewing movement.

Lee's feet slipped on the rain-wet deck. She tightened her grip on the railing, clung with all her strength as the weight of her body pulled her toward the bow. When she was standing again, her legs trembled beneath her and her anger was cold and hard as a glacier.

She should have fought them to a standstill at the dock. She should have run to the police office and cried that they were taking out the *Sue Belle* and only madmen and murderers would put to sea in a storm like this. Surely the police chief would have held them.

Now it was too late, probably forever too late. When the *Sue Belle* broke apart in the violence of the sea, Lee, before the last wisp of breath surrendered to the cold water, would bear the burden of Johnny's soul. He was only a boy. She should have prevented this mad expedition. The responsibility was hers, the blame. She brought Johnny and his story of the pretty girl all alone on that anchored boat to Dan's attention.

They were no more than out the door of the police station when Dan started in on Johnny. What was this about a girl?

What had she looked like? Where had Johnny seen her? When?

Under Dan's expert probing, Johnny built up a picture of the girl. "Yeah, that's what she looked like," Johnny said, "and she was pretty."

Dan's face was grim. When he had seen that pathetic wet body in the glare of flashlights, nothing had been pretty.

"Can you find the place where the boat was anchored?" Dan asked him tensely.

The boy looked away from Dan, looked through the sharply slanting rain toward the channel and the water that rose and fell roughly. From where they stood, they saw men working to anchor boats solidly. Closer to them, men hammered boards over windows.

"There must be a pretty rough one coming in," Johnny said slowly.

"Do you have a fix on the spot?" Dan persisted.

Johnny nodded. "Yea, but in weather like this it would be tough to find."

"What do you have? RDF?"

Johnny nodded again. "Yeah. But that flag out there is a small craft warning. They don't put that flag out unless they mean business."

Dan looked tense. "It wouldn't take long to check."

"Wait," Lee interrupted sharply. "We have to do something about Miss Abbott. We don't have time to go to a treasure site and certainly not in weather like this."

Dan didn't quite ignore her but he dismissed her concern as unimportant. "We have to find where that boat was. That's where the treasure is."

"Damn the treasure," Lee was furious. "We have to find Miss Abbott!"

Dan shoved a hand through his thick reddish hair. "I appreciate your concern for this lady," he said in a dangerously polite voice, "but we don't know that anything's happened to her at all. The chief thinks she's fine."

"The chief is a fool," Lee replied and her voice was dangerously polite, as well. "No woman leaves her purse behind. Only an elephant could have ripped that telephone wire out 'accidentally' and, even so he'd have knocked down the wall at the same time. Someone drew those red lines on the old newspaper. If nothing's happened to her, where is she? Where is Miss Abbott, minus purse and car on this delightful summer day?"

Lee had never realized she could sound so much like a fishwife but, darn it, it worked. Johnny remembered his friend and Dan, perforce, drove them to Miss Abbott's house.

It was a small frame built on stilts. No light shone from it as they pulled into the neat shell drive. Lee knew the visit was hopeless but she got out of the car anyway and hurried to the yellow-painted steps. She knocked on the screen door. The door rattled in its frame but all else was quiet. Lee heard rain water gushing from the spouts. In the distance the fog horn sounded its mournful cry.

Lee pulled open the screen and tried the doorknob. The knob turned. She pushed in the door and stepped into the tiny living room. A lacquered screen from China gleamed softly. It was a comfortable room with rattan furniture, a collection of daguerreotypes, and an easel with a seascape displayed.

Johnny came in behind her. "Is she here?" he asked hopefully.

Lee shook her head without turning. She finished the search, looking in the kitchen, the pale-yellow bathroom, the beige-and-lime bedroom. They went back to the car without talking.

Once inside the VW, Lee asked the boy, "Do you know her friends, her family? Anyone we could call and ask?"

That was when she lost control.

Dan beat down the idea of a search for Miss Abbott. "The woman obviously never locks up anything. Look at the front door of her house. You twist the knob and walk right in. What makes the shop different?"

"For one thing," she glared at him, "it's a store and stores are locked when closed."

But Johnny listened to Dan and slowly began to nod. After all even the chief thought that probably something had come up, some friend had called Miss Abbott away. It wasn't like they'd found any signs of a struggle or anything.

All this while, Lee was driving the VW back toward the shop and the waterfront and the *Sue Belle*. On the dock, Johnny finally acquiesced. The *Sue Belle*, even in her slip, was pitching up and down. Lee looked at the white caps racing in the channel and at the warning flag snapping wetly in the wind. She clutched at Johnny.

"This is crazy." She yelled to be heard above the wind and rain.

Johnny was shamefaced but stubborn, too. He wasn't going to let a girl, even a pretty girl who had befriended him, make him look like a chicken in front of a guy like Dan. "This isn't so bad, I've got a good fix. I found it easy as pie before." He turned and jumped onto the *Sue Belle*. Dan landed heavily right behind him. She stared after them and knew they would go, with or without her, so she jumped aboard, too.

Now, holding onto the railing with both hands, drenched through by the sharply slanting rain, she knew she had been a fool. Was there a patron saint for fools?

The *Sue Belle* staggered down into a trough, began her labored ascent.

Lee waited until the instant when the boat was level then she pushed away from the railing and flung herself across the deck and grabbed at the cabin housing. The *Sue Belle* made her lurching sashay from port to starboard. As the boat made another bow whacking descent, Lee pushed the sliding door wide enough to squeeze inside, caught at a bench near the door as the *Sue Belle* plunged.

Lee's progress through the aft cabin to the companionway leading up to the flying bridge was a series of rushes and abrupt stops. She reached the stairs, pulled herself up them. At the top, she stood still and stared out one of the broad sweeps of glass at the trough directly confronting the *Sue Belle*. The boat tipped forward. The rushing descent terrified her. She grabbed at a wooden slat holding a life preserver.

The deck tilted down and down and it took all her strength to hold on as the bow tilted down and the screws came up and hung free on the crest, whirling uselessly in the air. The *Sue Belle* began to yaw. After a heart stopping moment, she began to pull up her nose and the screws again moved in their element.

Johnny was sweating. Sweat rolled down his face. He swiped his arm across his face and squinted at the compass. He eased the speed and the *Sue Belle* slowed.

Lee timed her move and dashed to stand beside him, clinging as well as she could to the ribbed frame between windows.

He gave her one swift glance then looked back to the windows that gave onto the swift running sea.

"Tell Dan it'll take a little longer than I thought," the boy said tensely. "I had to slow down. The *Sue Belle* could broach at that speed. But we aren't far now. Maybe another fifteen minutes."

"The weather's worsening isn't it?" she demanded.

He held tight to the wheel and stared grimly out at the huge waves and the blackening sky. 'We're almost there."

"Johnny, go back."

He ignored her. This was not the boy with whom she had dealt, however briefly, on shore. This sweaty, taut-faced young man, eyes straining to see, shoulder muscles bunching as he gripped the wheel, was intent upon a course. Nothing was going to deflect him.

Lee turned away. It was a little easier to walk now. She thought bitterly that if she had known a little less speed would make this kind of difference she would have been up on the bridge much sooner. Now she could move, unsteadily but without holding on, to the companionway. She moved down the steps. At their base, she turned right and walked into the forward cabin. Dan was sitting on a wooden bench, neatly coiling an immensely long length of nylon rope.

"You look quite sporting" Lee said

He looked up his gray eyes remote, then down again at the line.

She realized he was a much bigger man than she had thought. In the brief blue trunks it was clear just how big he was, the breadth of his shoulders, the heavily muscled chest with its matted covering of reddish hair. In his shabby, somewhat ill-fitting clothes, he gave an impression of softness. There was nothing soft about him.

"Dan, "she said after a moment, "are you being fair to Johnny?"

This caught his attention. He looked up. The gray eyes didn't warm, but they were thoughtful.

"It isn't fair to risk his boat just to find treasure."

He looked past her, out the window at the foam-veined waves. He had never, of course, dived in weather like this, into water like this. It would be fatally easy to make a mistake. To get lost. In the rain, there was no more than twenty yards visibility. Twenty-five yards away the boat couldn't be seen. Of course, the fog whistle sounded and sounded but sound does funny things out on water especially to a swimmer down in the water.

He looked out at the savage sea and smiled without humor. "That wouldn't be fair," he said finally. He leaned down and strapped a knife to his leg.

"We'll go back then?" she asked eagerly.

He shook his head. "Not yet" and picked up the flashlight and pushed the button and looked at the bright gleam of light. He laid the flashlight aside and checked the other items piled by him, the regulator, float, flippers, depth gauge, weight belt, and the nylon line.

He studied the end of the line. It would be better if he had a metal snap for the end. If he couldn't find one, he'd better remember how to tie a good knot, the very best knot. The equipment was all right. Now it was time to check the anchor. He got up and started for the bow. "Will you give me hand with the anchor?"

He was almost to the doorway when she answered. "No."

He took another step. Paused, looked back "What?"

"I said no."

He stared at her for a moment. His reddish face flushed. "Suit yourself," and he walked on.

She hurried to the bridge. Ignoring Johnny's dark frown, she said, "Don't let Dan Holloway take advantage of you. He doesn't care about you or the *Sue Belle*. He'll do anything to find that treasure."

The boy gripped the wheel and stared out at the heaving water. Sweat glistened on his face. He breathed like he'd been running for a long time. He rubbed his right hand on his jeans, gripped the wheel again. "Yeah," Johnny said quietly. "I guess anybody who'll go down on a day like this will pretty much do anything if they think it's their job." He paused. "Dr. Holloway, he feels mighty bad about that girl. He feels like he has to do it. I told him it was crazy. I told him he could drown easy."

Lee felt very cold suddenly, very empty. She asked, pushing the words out of a dry throat, "Why? Why does he feel he has to?"

Johnny was watching the compass. He swung the *Sue Belle* a little to starboard. He flicked her a quick look, a puzzled look, "Cause she's dead. He feels like it's his fault because he saw the pin, tried to make her tell him about the pin." The boy frowned and reached out toward the RDF. "I'm close now. I must almost be on it." He looked again at Lee. "You see, if he can take a piece of the treasure back to Port Aransas, the chief will believe him and the police will start looking for the guy who really killed her. Dr. Holloway feels like he owes her that. And he has to dive now because if it's a real blow coming there won't be any treasure to find tomorrow. By the time a storm gets through everything down there could be covered with ten feet of sand and there wouldn't ever be any way to prove there was a treasure."

Lee was halfway down the companionway when the motor stopped. She had thought the *Sue Belle* tossed when she was under way, but it was nothing to the tremendous roll and pitch when the motor was stilled and the boat was at the mercy of the waves.

Catching hold here, clinging there, she made her way to Dan at the bow. He was kneeling by the windlass. He signaled to Johnny and the *Sue Belle*'s engine started and the boat reversed.

"Steady," Dan shouted. "That's good." Once again the motor stopped. The *Sue Belle* immediately surged up and down, but there was a feeling of control and Lee no longer felt convinced a watery grave was imminent.

At least, not for her.

Dan still knelt by the bow, one hand gripping the anchor line.

The cold stinging rain swept over them. He stared at the heaving Gulf. Then he reached up to pull down the face mask.

Lee touched his arm and she could feel the tension in his muscles, in his bones.

He looked around, startled.

"I'm sorry," she shouted. "I didn't understand."

For a moment, the cool gray eyes were still remote, then a smile flickered on his face. "That's okay. To be honest, my motives are a little mixed." He thought for a moment and grinned hugely. "Think what a dramatic obituary it will make in the museum bulletin." But the grin didn't reach those eyes, those eyes she was beginning to know. She understood then just how dreadful the dive was going to be.

She stared at him, then on an impulse she didn't probe, scarcely wanted to probe, she leaned forward and caught that angular face between her hands and kissed him. She kissed him as if a night had just begun, and there was all the time in the world and only the two of them.

CHAPTER 17

Dan moved hand over hand down the anchor line. Only his tight grip kept him from being swept away. In shallows such as these, storm waves tumble the water all the way to the bottom. He turned the light of the flash onto his depth gauge. Nine feet. Ten. He stopped, hung on with his left hand, clamped his nose shut with his right hand, blew to clear his ears. He continued his descent into the swirling water. No visibility today. As the water buffeted, he knew it would be a miracle to find anything even if there were anything to find. What were the odds that a kid like Johnny could manage in this kind of ocean to bring a boat right on a fix? Not high.

Twenty feet down, he stopped and blew again. At twenty-seven feet, he reached bottom. He gripped the *Sue Belle*'s anchor chain and stared into turbid water. Even with the flashlight, visibility was less than a foot.

Was he wasting his time? Should he instead be trying to find Harry Cassell, the elusive scuba diving resident of Nightingale Courts, who went fishing at nine o'clock last night? Maybe he should have been wiser to head straight for Aransas Pass the minute he got out of the police station.

This effort looked hopeless. Damn hopeless. He grimly

wrapped his left leg around the anchor chain so that both hands would be free. He was down here. He would look.

He needed both hands now because this had to be done right. He slipped the loops of nylon line off his right shoulder took the end with a metal snap attached and gave it a viciously hard tug.

The snap held.

He yanked again. The metal fastener stayed on the end of the line, He held it in his hand and rubbed his thumb against it. The snap was a small piece of metal to trust with his life.

He snapped the metal fastener to the anchor chain and started off. With the line running out over his right shoulder he swam forward. He aimed the beam of the flashlight at the ocean floor. He struggled to stay near the bottom, battling the storm-fueled currents to keep a straight course.

He was tired even before he reached the end of his fifty-foot line. He turned to his left, keeping the line taut, and began to cover the outer edge of his circle. He was perhaps halfway around when the line fell slack. He stopped. His legs dropped until he stood amid the dark sandy buffeting water, holding the limp line in his hand.

If the snap had pulled free from the anchor chain, he was a dead man.

He couldn't judge how long he stood, blood drumming in his ears. He fought and mastered the frantic desire to surface to get up and out of the dark water. If he surfaced, it wasn't likely he'd ever find the *Sue Belle*.

Feeling his heart squeeze, he started to coil the rope. He circled the line about his hand once, twice, a third time. The fourth time there was resistance. The relief was so overwhelming that he felt weak. He waited a moment more before resuming his search yanking several times on the line. Why had the rope hung limp for that heart-stopping interval?

"Stupid," he said to himself silently. Somebody as stupid as he didn't deserve a lifeline. Sure the line had gone soft. He was moving along the circumference of a circle and his line was limited to fifty feet. But the center of the circle, the anchor chain, was moveable. Obviously, the *Sue Belle* had swung about, moving the anchor chain nearer him and causing a sudden slack in his line. His chagrin propelled him faster. He bulled his way through the turbulent water. When he judged that he'd been around the perimeter all the way, he looped up two feet of line and began to look closer in. If that yielded nothing, he'd pull in another two feet and try again. He was trained to patience and he was a stubborn man. He was going to search until further search was hopeless. Or impossible.

He looked at his watch when he finished the second circuit. Forty minutes. He was very tired. The water was a constant pressure but he looped up another two feet and began again. A rough surge caught him by surprise midway through the third circuit. The force of the sweep tumbled him onto the sandy bottom, turning him head over heels, but, he kept his vise-tight grip on the line. He had his priorities firmly in mind.

He slammed hard against the bottom. His feet tangled in a mass of sea weed. He was kicking free when his right knee scraped painfully against something sharp and rocky. He yanked at the seaweed for an instant before his heart lurched. There are no rocks off the Texas coast. The ocean floor is sandy, free of coral, free of rocks, a shallow shelf that runs far out into the Gulf.

Sea shells.

He dropped to the bottom, flashed the light back and forth, His free hand swept groped, searching, The minute his hand closed around the shell-encrusted stone ball, he knew what he'd found. A neon sign couldn't proclaim a wreck half so well. All the old ships carried stone ballast balls. When a ship went down to the sea for the final time, the hull split open and ballast balls tumbled out to lie for centuries.

Dan held the ballast ball in his hand. He had proof now. No man could question this. He found its weight an aid against the surging beat of the water. It was getting rougher all the time. He'd better get back up to the *Sue Belle*.

He crouched by a thick cluster of ballast balls and was pumped with energy. He'd found a galleon from the hurricane of 1553. The pin he'd seen on Judy's blouse was more magnificent than the proudest exhibits in the grandest museums. What else might be here?

The swift currents threatened to knock him off his feet. It was getting harder all the time to keep his balance against the buffeting water. The wave action was obviously increasing. He wondered at the edge of his mind how the *Sue Belle* was riding. But he didn't worry. It might be uncomfortable aboard her, even a little frightening, but she was seaworthy. She could take a lot more. This was a passing judgment, a peripheral thought, for his mind was intent upon what the increasing violence of the sea might do to the site. In his mind, the discovery was already a site. Heavy seas could pummel the low-lying mounds of debris and tomorrow the contour of the bottom could be two feet higher or lower and all the remains covered or scattered.

He fought the ebb and surge of the water and moved slowly, watching for heavy encrustations of shells on odd-shaped mounds. Normally, of course, he wouldn't dream of disturbing a site, but if he could find and salvage anything now, he should. By tomorrow everything lying here might be gone. He couldn't stay down much longer. In the few remaining minutes, he would search.

Aboard the *Sue Belle*, the storm was worse and had been

growing steadily worse for the past half hour. Lee made coffee. The task didn't absorb nearly enough time or attention. When she poured a steaming cup for Johnny, the *Sue Belle* made one of her more spectacular sideways plunges and the hot liquid splashed over the rim of the cup and onto her hand. She poured cold water over the burn and wished that it was the pain which caused the tears to slide down her face. But she knew better.

After she carried the cup to Johnny, she made her way back to the galley but her own coffee grew cold and she finally poured it out. A hot liquid wouldn't touch the ice in her heart. She stumbled out on the deck and held to the bow rail and watched the anchor chain. Two years ago, she might have hoped. She no longer had confidence in life. It took so little to destroy it. A burst of anti-aircraft fire and a huge helicopter fell in flames, all aboard killed. What hope was there for a quixotic diver submerged in a heaving sea?

The rain pelted her but she stayed at the bow. How long had Dan been gone? She didn't know. She moved past the narrow stretch of deck alongside the cabin housing. When she could see the after deck she grabbed at the railing and jerked to a stop.

For a moment, she thought she'd gone mad. It was impossible. There simply could not be a stranger standing on the deck no more than four feet from her, a stranger with gun in hand, pointing the gun at her. He loomed only a few feet away. Tawny blond hair was molded to his heavy head by the pelting rain. His face was broad with a short nose and wide-spaced eyes and blunt jaw. He stood with his feet wide apart, his shoulders hunched forward.

Lee knew Dan wouldn't have to search for Harry Cassell. He was here. The treasure seeker. The killer.

She stepped back one pace and then another.

He was not terribly big. Not as tall as Dan. But he was powerfully built. He moved inexorably closer.

She retreated until her back was hard against the cabin housing.

He loomed over her.

She knew she faced death.

His full mouth twisted in anger. “What are you doing here?”

She stood wordless.

“This is the boat that kept nosing around all week and some kid talked to Judy. I thought I fixed him up for good. I thought they'd take his boat away when they found cocaine.” There was hatred in his eyes. “What are you doing here? You don't have any right here.”

He raised his arm and she saw the shining black metal of the gun and knew he was going to batter it down against her head.

“Hey, Lee.” It was a triumphant shout, a conquering shout.

The gun sliced down through the air and Harry pressed the barrel against her throat.

Dan shouted again from the bow. This time a hint of impatience edged his voice. He was a victor awaiting his laurel.

Harry nodded toward the bow and prodded her with the gun then stepped back a pace to let her move free from the cabin housing.

“Lee,” Dan shouted “come here. I found the galleon. I've brought up a piece—” He broke off as she came stiffly in view. He could not yet see Harry coming behind her. But the exhilaration of surviving that foolhardy dive, the sheer excitement of his find had thrown everything into high relief. He knew at once that something was wrong and took a step toward her.

Lee saw the obviously heavy, plate-shaped, shell-encrusted mass that he held in his hands and she seized the moment. The

Sue Belle was beginning the elephantine down-dip of the bow. Lee half fell to the left.

Harry stopped short and swung the gun from her toward Dan. Then Lee grabbed at his arm, pulling the gun down and screaming all the while, "Throw it at him, Dan. Throw it."

There was an instant, a tiny fraction of time, when he could have moved and swung the relic, thrown the heavy sharp-edged mass at Harry.

But some things a man can do and some he can't. To give Dan his due, Lee never doubted his motive. It wasn't fear of the gun that held his aim. It wasn't the motionless response of shock. Dan responded right enough. He understood well enough and quickly enough. But he held a treasure in his hand, a survival of time past. He leaned forward quickly to lay down the ungainly block and in one swift motion rose and was moving across the deck and reaching for the knife on his leg.

Harry grabbed her, threw her to the deck. Now he leaned forward pressing the gun against the back of her head.

Dan read her death warrant in Harry's eyes and so he stopped.

Slowly, Harry lifted the gun from her and pointed it toward Dan.

Harry gave Lee a kick. "Get up. "He never took his eyes off Dan.

Her arm was bruised by the kick. Her knee hurt from striking the deck. She slowly pulled herself up, glared at Dan. Damn his archeological soul to hell.

CHAPTER 18

Lee led the way toward the companionway. She moved with leaden steps. A killer with a gun followed and they had no way to stop him. Harry Cassell was alert, watchful. She wondered how long he would bother to keep them alive. He could easily shoot them, toss their bodies into the Gulf. Lee held to the railing, pulled herself up a step at a time. Dan followed her. Harry Cassell was behind them.

Lee stepped through the doorway, and Dan was close behind her.

A thud.

She whirled. Johnny grappled with Harry. Johnny should have cracked the top of Harry's head with a gaff. He should have looped line around his throat. Instead he jumped him like a tackle on the high school football team.

Dan lunged forward but the heavy tank still strapped to his back slowed him.

Harry brought up a knee. As Johnny gasped for air and clutched his stomach, Harry leveled the gun at him. He flicked a thumb at Lee. "Get a rope." He trained the gun on Dan. "You move and she's dead. And the kid, too."

It didn't take long. A miserable Johnny weakly directing

her to a locker, Lee pulling out a coil of nylon rope. Following Harry's instructions, she tied Johnny to a railing at the side of the bridge.

All the while, the barrel of the gun pointed at Dan's head and it didn't waver. Their stocky captor breathed heavily. Sweat trickled down his face even though it was chilly and damp. His eyes flickered toward Lee. "Is there anybody else on board?"

Lee quickly shook her head, then wondered if she should have lied, if she had lost some advantage by her honest reply. In almost the same instant, she was irritated at her academic analysis. The point was moot. She had to focus on what they could do now. If anything.

Harry slowly nodded.

Lee found his empty face frightening. He never changed expression.

He gestured at Lee. "You come here." He was staring at Lee. When she didn't move, he pointed the gun at her. "You come here."

She walked reluctantly toward him. When she was within reach, he grabbed her arm and yanked her close and jabbed the gun muzzle hard against her head. Then he looked at Dan. "Now you listen," Harry said in his soft and uninflected voice. "I don't want any more trouble. If you give me any trouble, I'm going to blow her head off."

Lee closed her eyes briefly. When she opened them in a moment and looked across the room, she saw hard ridges of muscle in Dan's face and the thin tight line of his mouth. She wondered if her face was as pale as his.

It was very quiet in the cabin. The wind shrilled outside and the rain splatted down and the water curled and hissed but inside the cabin the only noise was Harry Cassell's heavy breaths. "Okay now," Harry said more easily. "First, you take off that tank real careful and lay it on the deck."

When Dan carefully, slowly put down the tank, Harry nodded. "That's real good. Now, we'll go aft. I got some things I want to bring on board. You'll do the bringing," his big head nodded toward Dan. "If you try any tricks, your girl won't be around to see them."

When they stood in the pelting rain on the after deck, Lee wasn't surprised to see the rain-shrouded motor boat securely tied to a bitt and bobbing up and down at the end of a line.

Lee stared curiously at the boat. Today was Sunday. Last Friday the sun had glittered on a June-blue Gulf and a pretty dark-haired girl had sat in the back of that boat and held a fishing rod.

Harry nodded at Dan. "Pull the boat in close enough so you can jump on board. Untie the old lady, get her on board."

Lee drew in a quick breath. The old lady. Could he possibly mean Miss Abbott? Could Miss Abbott be on that lurching motorboat? She twisted her face to look up at Harry. "Is it Miss Abbott?"

The gun stayed hard against her head. He flicked a quick look at her. "The lady from the antique shop," he said. "She's going to help me sell my treasure." He talked on, almost happily. He had it all figured out, a truck into Mexico, Miss Abbott to translate and to lead the way to the dealer in Mexico City.

Lee's throat was suddenly dry. He had figured out how to sell his treasure and there was no place in his plans for Dan or Johnny or her. What was he going to do with them?

Harry stopped talking when Dan pulled the motor boat close to the stern of the *Sue Belle* and wrapped the slack in the line around the bitt. Then he got up and grabbed the railing and looked over the stern.

"Don't jump," Lee screamed. "You can't make it."

"Shut up," Harry said viciously and he shook her as a dog might shake a rabbit.

Lee pressed the back of her hand against her mouth. Dan couldn't jump.

Dan climbed carefully over the railing. He leaned forward knees bent, and watched the high foam-flecked waves, trying to judge a pattern, a system. When he jumped, she closed her eyes and didn't breathe. She listened. And heard a shout.

"Yo." A pause. "Stand by. I need some help."

Lee pulled away from Harry and hurried to the stern. Harry followed but he didn't try to grab her again.

Lee bent over the railing, saw the small trussed figure near Dan's feet. "Miss Abbott are you all right?"

Dan crouched in the cockpit to cut the ropes. He helped the older woman to her feet. She clung to him and looked across the writhing water at Lee.

"I'm fine, thank you, my dear." Her sandy hair was awry, her knit dress a sagging mess, but her voice rang clear and sweet and undiminished.

"Hurry up," Harry yelled.

Lee could feel the fierce and dangerous emotions that pulsed in him.

"Throw me another rope," Dan called.

Lee hurried to the forward cabin and found the coil of nylon line Dan had used in his dive. She brought the rope to the stern.

"Tie the rope to the railing," Dan directed.

Lee pushed her wet hair back from her face, tried to dry her hands on her slacks but they were sopping. The rope was as slippery and unmanageable as a handful of wet spaghetti, but she worked as quickly as she could. When the rope was knotted around the stanchion, she pulled on it with all her strength. Finally, she flung the end across the tormented water. Dan grabbed the coil. In a quick movement, he tied the line around Miss Abbott's waist.

Lee stared down at the gap between the boats and the surging foaming water. The motor of the smaller craft rumbled.

Harry raised his arm and pointed the gun. Then, slowly, the tension eased out of his arm.

Dan backed the motor boat until the line linking it to the *Sue Belle* stretched straight and taut in the air. Then he nodded at Miss Abbott.

It took a magnificent amount of seamanship. Dan held the nose of the motor boat into the waves and fed her just enough gas to keep the line taut. Too much and the strain might break the line. Too little and it would drop into the sea.

It took a magnificent amount of courage on the part of Miss Abbott. She gripped the rope and started swinging hand over hand. Lee looked at the long length of rope and could almost feel the socket-wrenching strain on Miss Abbott's arms.

Once a steep wave pulled hungrily at her legs, but doggedly, grimly, Lee knew it was a triumph of will over muscle, the kind of will that claws and kicks and fights every last inch of the way.

Lee climbed over the edge of the railing and hung precariously out over the water, gripping the railing with her left arm reaching forward and down for Miss Abbott with her right. When she could grip the older woman's arm, she pulled and hauled and helped until Miss Abbott was safely on the deck.

The engine of the motor boat cut off. Dan shouted "The rope. Throw it to me and I'll try to rig a line to transfer the treasure."

Dan brought the ice chest out of the cockpit and tied the line around it, sling fashion.

Harry leaned across the railing, directing, ordering, berating. He didn't trust the sling. Dan frowned and stared down at it and nodded in agreement. For the moment, they were not captor and captive but disgruntled collaborators, unable to achieve their objective. Lee wondered if Harry realized that Dan in his own fashion was as absorbed by the treasure and its transfer as Harry.

The wind howled now and all the waves were froth crested. The rain swept in an icy torrent.

The men despaired of a safe sling. Dan tried powering the *Lucky Lady* close enough to the *Sue Belle* for Harry to haul the chests across only a short span. But it was too rough. The smaller craft almost broached twice. A third time, sheer luck kept the motor boat from smashing into the *Sue Belle*'s stern.

With each frustration, Harry grew a little wilder, a little more dangerous. Miss Abbott watched with a worried frown.

When the *Lucky Lady* swerved away from the final near disaster, Dan yelled "Look, the only safe thing is a tow. In this kind of ocean, a tow will help stabilize the *Sue Belle*, too. The treasure will be perfectly safe. We'll pull the *Lucky Lady* into Corpus Christi."

"That's quite true, Harry. I think that's a good idea," Miss Abbott said briskly.

Lee was surprised at how he accepted her comment, as if from an ally, and how her support calmed him.

Dan pulled the ice chest back into the cockpit of the *Lucky Lady* and even Harry couldn't question the care Dan took in retying the chest.

Then it was time for Dan to come back aboard the *Sue Belle.*

Harry raised the gun ever so slightly. Lee saw the thought in his stolid face. She tightened up inside, getting ready to spring, knowing it would be the last thing she would ever do. Knowing it. Accepting it.

Harry lowered the gun. Such a small movement to mean so much.

She watched him carefully, however, as Dan tied one end of the rope around his waist. He would not have a line to swing hand over hand to safety because there was no one to maneuver the *Lucky Lady* and keep the line taut for Dan.

He poised on the bow of the *Lucky Lady*, jumped into the roiling water and began to swim. The waves moved him up and down like a twig in a torrent. He was a powerful swimmer but this was no water for a swimmer. And he was tired the dark and dangerous dive, the piloting of the motor boat, the struggle to transfer the treasure. Now the waves heaved him up and tumbled him down. Then a cross-wave surged from his right, lifted him up and flung him toward the side of the *Sue Belle.*

CHAPTER 19

Lee knew it would be easy to give up, to rest her face against the slick varnished wood of the deck and let happen what would. But the small kink of rope wedged between her wrists demanded response.

Lee's eyes were closed and once again she remembered that dreadful moment when the wave threw Dan against the side of the *Sue Belle*. Harry roughly pulled on the rope and hauled Dan up the side and over the railing.

When Dan fell to the deck, Lee hurried to him and knelt, then helped him slowly to his feet. Blood ran down his face from a gash over one eye. His left arm hung at an odd angle. Lines of pain splayed out from his mouth but she knew they were lucky he could stand there at all.

Harry had been impatient. "You can handle the wheel with one hand," and it was an order, not a question. Then he had stared at Lee and Miss Abbott.

"Come on,"and he motioned them toward the cabin housing. Once inside, he commanded Dan to tie them up. Dan's left arm was almost useless but he saw the wild and restive look in Harry's eyes so he tied them and managed to make it look firm and tight even though he tucked the little extra kink of rope between Lee's wrists.

When Harry and Dan left to go to the bridge, Miss Abbott looked at her. "Where is Johnny?"

"He's tied up too. On the bridge."

They were quiet then. Lee lay on the hard deck and wearily knew she must try to get free. She opened her eyes and looked at Miss Abbott and realized the older woman's faded blue eyes were searching the cabin intently.

"There is cutlery in the galley" Miss Abbott said. "Perhaps, if I rolled over there I could get a knife."

Suddenly Lee didn't feel quite so near defeat. "Wait a minute. Dan put a little slack in the rope around my wrist. Let me see if I can get free. You watch for Harry."

Lee twisted her wrists. She pulled. She strained. She wriggled. Nothing seemed to spread the bonds. The extra kink stayed stubbornly wedged between her wrists.

Miss Abbott awkwardly rolled herself closer. "Let me see what I can do."

They lay back to back and Lee felt Miss Abbott's fingers tugging at the loop. Miss Abbott was a patient woman. Long after Lee had despaired, the older woman kept pulling and tugging and finally, abruptly, Lee felt the rope slacken.

She worked desperately after that. If Harry came to check and she was only half free, it would all be for nothing. Their effort would probably be for nothing anyway. How she could possibly disarm and capture Harry was a little beyond her imaginings. But she was trying and she would keep on trying because Miss Abbott wouldn't give up and Dan, obviously, never knew when he was licked. Lee had a fairly good idea the game was over but, nevertheless, when her hands were free she pulled herself across the floor to the galley and managed to stand and open the cutlery drawer and get a knife. She sliced the rope from around her ankles, then stumbled across the cabin to Miss Abbott.

When the older woman was free and sitting up and rubbing her ankles, Lee faced the door, knife in hand. And wondered wildly what she was going to do. She had to do something, mount some sort of attack. Her only hope was surprise. She didn't even notice that Miss Abbott had struggled to her feet and was moving unsteadily toward the cutlery drawer.

Lee crept up the companionway. She paused near the top step.

Dan's voice was insistent. "I have to slow her down. We're going to tear her bottom out if we try to keep up this speed."

"Have you got a course figured for Corpus?"

Lee dared to move higher and look onto the bridge and then she stood, terrified.

Dan was nodding and pointing to the chart clamped down to his left. "If we keep to this course, we shouldn't have any trouble."

Harry's head nodded thoughtfully. His arm with the gun began to rise and Lee knew Harry had decided he no longer needed Dan.

She moved then. She ran, the knife held high.

He heard her, of course, and began to turn and the gun swung toward her.

She plunged the knife down. The blade jarred against Harry's elbow and sliced his forearm open from elbow to wrist. The shocking spurt of bright red blood splattered over her and the deck. The gun clattered down onto the deck.

She could never separate what happened next: the blow that struck her in the shoulder; Dan's shout; the sudden, horrifying plunge of the *Sue Belle* swinging out of control; the vicious, ugly struggle of the two men; and her own pain-filled scrabbling across the deck toward the gun.

But she would never forget the stern yet sad call from the door. "Harry, the rope has broken. The *Lucky Lady* is pulling away. Oh, do come quickly."

With the strength of the possessed, Harry flung Dan against the console and turned toward Miss Abbott.

"The rope has broken," she said again.

Harry swayed on his feet, his light blue eyes glazed with pain. Blood dripped steadily in a thick rivulet from his split mouth and spurted from his arm. As Lee grabbed up the gun and ran to Dan, Harry staggered past then, heading toward the companionway.

The *Sue Belle* tipped far to port.

Miss Abbott finished cutting Johnny's ropes and he rolled to his feet and rushed to the wheel.

Dan plunged across the cabin, heading for the deck.

Lee, too, moved toward the companionway. It was easier now because Johnny had the *Sue Belle* back under control. The boat slowed, steadied despite the heavy seas.

Lee and Dan reached the stern in time to see the *Lucky Lady* slowly turning sideways to the force of a monstrous wave.

Harry gave a wordless shout and pulled himself up on the railing and dived into the roiling violence of the water. He swam awkwardly with his good arm toward the *Lucky Lady* and then an immense wave washed over him. He did not come to the surface. Another huge wave crested and the motor boat was no longer visible.

EPILOGUE

Lee unlocked the narrow-grilled gate, fished the mail out of the box and dumped it in the top of her market basket. She hummed cheerfully—albeit somewhat tunelessly—as she pulled the gate shut behind her and hurried up the red glazed tile walk toward the house.

The maid heard her coming and opened the front door, "Ah senora, the luncheon will be ready soon."

"There's no hurry," Lee said happily. She carried the shopping basket to the kitchen and would have puttered amiably about, putting things away, but she knew that Maria considered la cocina her domain. It still seemed to Lee that for two impecunious academics their quarters were extravagant in the extreme but it was only for the summer and, compared to American rents, it was theirs for a moderate sum.

She took the little stack of mail from the top of the basket and returned to the central hallway and walked to the sunroom and a back door that opened onto a tiny but incredibly lovely garden. Bougainvillea spilled down the sides of the rock walls. A weeping willow swept the ground in one corner and a hammock was stretched between two palms trees.

Lee walked on the flagstones to the hammock and sat

down. She flicked through the mail. The New Republic, SR, Expedition, a letter to Dan from St. Louis. Lee looked at the return addressee, Chrissa Melton. Hmm. She added it to the magazines and looked at the other letter and smiled. A letter addressed to Mrs. Daniel Holloway.

Lee settled back in the hammock, then opened her letter and pulled out several sheets filled with firm neat handwriting and read:

Dear Lee,

I was so pleased to hear from you and to learn that all is going well. The house does indeed sound lovely and Colima is, I understand, a very beautiful small city.

Most of the hurricane damage has been cleared away but Port Aransas still looks a bit ravaged. However, we have picked ourselves up from worse blows so I know it will all come right. We were, of course, so fortunate to reach Corpus Christi before the hurricane struck. I am also grateful that the damage to Of Things Past was minimal. I had to put in all new plate glass and replace much of the roof, but had little water damage.

There is still a good deal of excitement and discussion about our adventure with the treasure. Aransas Pass is filled with eager treasure hunters. Johnny takes the Sue Belle out whenever possible to scuba dive and search for the Lucky Lady. Since the RDF was smashed when Dan and Harry fought and we couldn't get a fix where Harry was lost, there's no way of even guessing where we were with any precision.

As for the original galleon site, the hurricane apparently redistributed the sand to such an extent that nothing has been found yet. The University team, however, is continuing to search.

I know this will be a glorious summer for you and Dan, and I do think you made such a wise decision. I ever agree with Horace: Seize now and here the hour that is, nor trust some later day!

My very best wishes to you in your new life.
Your friend,
Evelyn

Then Lee heard the front gate squeak and she tossed down the letter and pulled up out of the hammock and ran to meet him.

He hurried through the back door into the garden and wrapped his good arm around her. "Have you kept out of trouble while I've been off diligently scooping dirt out of a trench?"

"I've been diligent as well. I finished updating the list of excavated items, then I went marketing. The major excitement is the arrival of the mail. We have a very nice letter from Miss Abbott."

She walked to the hammock and gathered up the mail and handed it to him. "Oh yes, there's a letter for you from the museum."

He glanced at it. "A monthly report. That can wait." He opened Miss Abbott's letter, read it, looked inquiringly at his wife. "I hope, Mrs. Holloway, that you heartily agree marrying me was a 'wise' thing to do?"

She grinned and said lightly, "I don't know how wise it was." She paused a beat, added, "But it's certainly fun."

He pulled her down onto the hammock with him. "That's the proper attitude," he commended. He kissed her, not lightly at all.

In a moment, she said in a slightly muffled voice, "Maria has lunch almost ready and you have to go back to the dig."

"Not until after siesta." He lifted his head and frowned. "But I do have to see about a new foreman. The last anybody saw of ours, he was disappearing into the sunset with a crate of tequila." Dan sat up and, with his left arm still in a sling, maneuvered himself gingerly out of the hammock. "We better have lunch and I'll see to the new foreman. But, after siesta, why don't you come on down to the dig. I want to show you what we found this morning."

Lee walked into the house with him, his good arm around her shoulders. She smiled up at her lanky, red-mustached, determined, charming, obdurate partner. Wise? Oh, yes. The only further wisdom she would ever need would be to remember never to come between an archeologist and his treasures, be they of clay, bone, stone or gold.

ABOUT THE AUTHOR

Carolyn Hart, an accomplished master of mystery, is the author of twenty previous Death on Demand novels. Her books have won multiple Agatha, Anthony, and Macavity Awards. She is also the creator of the Henrie O series which features a retired reporter, and the Bailey Ruth series which stars an impetuous, redheaded ghost. One of the founders of Sisters in Crime, Hart lives in Oklahoma City.

CAROLYN HART

FROM OPEN ROAD MEDIA

OPEN ROAD
INTEGRATED MEDIA

www.ingramcontent.com/pod-product-compliance
Lightning Source LLC
LaVergne TN
LVHW090606110826
845146LV00001B/287